Promises Kept

GIACOMO GIAMMATTEO

Also by Giacomo Giammatteo:

Fiction:
Friendship & Honor Series:
MURDER TAKES TIME: Friendship & Honor: Book I
MURDER HAS CONSEQUENCES: Friendship & Honor: Book II
MURDER TAKES PATIENCE: Friendship & Honor Book III

Blood Flows South Series:
A BULLET FOR CARLOS: Blood Flows South: Book I
FINDING FAMILY: Blood Flows South: the Beginning (A Novella)
A BULLET FROM DOMINIC: Blood Flows South: Book II

Redemption Series:
Necessary Decisions
Old Wounds

Non-Fiction:
No Mistakes Careers
NO MISTAKES RESUMES: Book One of No Mistakes Careers
NO MISTAKES INTERVIEWS: Book Two of No Mistakes Careers

Sanctuary Tales (True Stories From An Animal Sanctuary)
WHISKERS & BEAR (Coming soon)

Promises Kept

GIACOMO GIAMMATTEO

INFERNO PUBLISHING COMPANY

GRADUATION DAY

They say rookie cops have the best chance of getting killed the first year on the job. They say rookie cops are afraid to take a hit. They say rookie cops make all the mistakes. I heard all the talk, but no matter what they say, I say bullshit. No way this rookie cop was letting any of that happen.

Margie was voted most likely to make captain. Rodrigo got all the votes for desk sergeant and Jason for Rookie of the Year award. Me? I got voted most likely to kill someone in the first year. I had a gut feeling they were right.

I stood shoulder-to-shoulder with men and women I'd spent the past six months with. Six grueling months that transformed us from pure rookies into "official rookies." It was already ninety-two degrees, unusually hot for San Francisco, but I didn't move or let it bother me. The guy next to me didn't have the control; he wiped sweat from his brow for the third time.

Sergeant Baker glared at him from his spot at the side of the stage, where he stood guard and monitored who climbed the steps that led to the podium. Technically, he was there to congratulate us as we climbed the steps to accept our badges; I figured he was there to bust our ass one last time.

Captain Gerard Healy called out the names. Healy was a skinny little guy, no more than a hundred forty pounds, but his booming voice carried across the crowd without the help of a microphone. He also had a habit of butchering all but the most common names. The first name was easy, probably one of the reasons he chose it.

"Margie Jones."

Margie stood in the front row. She moved forward crisply, just like we practiced, and did a perfect "left face turn," marching until she reached Sergeant Baker, where she repeated her perfection with a "right face." Margie stood rigid as a statue; she appeared to be auditioning for the captain role already

Baker smiled and patted her back. She moved up the steps as if she were a robot, her lips pressed tightly together, refusing the smile that I knew was inside her. A gloating smile, at that.

She had graduated number one in the class and, as of this morning, she hadn't quit reminding us of that fact. It pissed off a lot of my classmates, but not me. Margie was so rigid, I figured she'd be the first one to get shot or die on the job.

Margie was book smart, but that wouldn't count. If there was one thing I knew beyond all else, cops without street smarts didn't survive, not in San Francisco.

Next, he called Rodrigo. He had put on ten pounds in the past few weeks. Looked like desk sergeant was a good option.

Next, Healy shouted for Jason, who damn near bounced up the steps, with more energy than a Duracell battery. He just might make rookie of the year, if he didn't jump off a cliff first.

Healy called out another name, a Japanese guy who had given Margie a run for the title of "most likely to make captain." A few more people got badges as the day grew hotter. I stared off into a beautiful blue sky and lost track of things.

"Lisa Benz," Healy called.

No one stepped forward, so he called again. "Lisa Benz."

Suddenly it hit me. Christ, that's me. I came alert with a jerk and moved out of line, making my way to the front. Baker wore a scowl, same as the one he greeted us with every morning during training.

"Sleeping, Benz?"

I smiled at him, the last thing he expected, but I didn't dare do anything else. There were two people ahead of me, waiting on the steps, eager to walk across the stage and get their badges. And that meant I was stuck beside Baker until they moved. I expected more shit from the sergeant, but he leaned close and whispered.

"Despite what you think, Benz. I like you. Stay safe out there, and call if you need anything."

I cocked my head to see if he was messing with me. He wasn't. This was real. "Thanks, Sarge. I just might do that."

"Lisa Benz," Healy called.

When I didn't budge, the sarge said, "In case you're wondering, that's you."

I flushed, but smiled and stepped onto the stage. People must have thought I was an idiot, not recognizing my name, but if they knew I'd stolen the ID from a dead girl not too long ago, then they'd understand.

As I walked across the stage toward Captain Healy, my mind raced. The day was finally here. In a few minutes, I was going to be a cop. A real cop. I hadn't planned on being a cop. Hadn't decided that until a few years ago, and even after I made up my mind, it was still iffy.

I had no idea how I'd get into the academy. I knew I could pass the physical part of the test, and I knew enough about cops from my time on the streets to pass the bullshit parts, but I had no idea how I'd pass the rest of the testing. I felt sure the questions were above an eighth-grade education. Worst of all, I had no idea how I'd get admitted without an ID. But that was before the dead girl.

Mick said God would give me a sign if he wanted me to go this route. I figured the dead girl was a "yes."

I listened as the captain went on and on about the proud

tradition of the SFPA and how excited he was that the top two graduates in each segment of the academy were women. With each bullshit sentence, I tried to imagine the next phase of my life.

I pictured myself riding shotgun in patrol cars, walking beats in the Mission District, or writing up countless tickets by Chinatown or North Beach. But most of all I imagined what it was going to feel like when I caught him. All I needed was a dark, lonely alley on a moonless night with a heavy layer of fog. That wasn't too much to ask for, not in SF. God and good fortune brought me this far. If He could give me that much, I'd take care of the rest.

As I thought more about it, I realized I intended to fulfill that prediction the class made when they voted me most likely to kill someone in the first year.

CHAPTER 1
FIRST MEMORIES

19 years ago, San Francisco.

I've heard it said that people who have strong memories from childhood are either blessed or cursed. I remember everything about my childhood, all the way back to when I was three years old.

##

I was running down the sidewalk wearing only my panties when I heard Mom's voice.

"Morgan, time to come in."

"Not yet."

"It's bath time," she said.

I stopped running and raced for the door to the apartment complex. "Hold that open," I hollered to one of the kids on our floor. I ran in and started up the stairs, letting out an "ouch" when a splinter jabbed my foot.

Bath time was my favorite time of day, at least on the days I got baths. Mom didn't always have time to help, and Rachel wasn't old enough, so whenever Mom did have time, I made sure not to miss it.

I banged on the front door of the apartment, stepping in place until Rachel opened it. "Hurry up," she said. "Mom's got the tub filled."

I tore off my panties as I went into the bathroom.

Mom looked at me with a sideways glance. "I see you were out playing without clothes again, young miss."

"Not for long," I said. "Maybe a minute."

"One minute is 'long,' and I'm sure it was more than that."

"One minute might be long to you," I said, "but not to me."

"Regardless, until Mr. Right comes along and provides a nice house in the suburbs, you dress before you go out and play."

I didn't know what she was talking about, but I said, "Okay, Mom."

One of the first memories I recall is of Mom bathing me in the tub, scrubbing me with a sponge and squeezing it to drip water on my back. I laughed, and then I begged her to do it again. After that, Mom would swish the water around real hard and make a whirlpool, and I'd drop a little floating frog in the water and watch it go round and round.

When we finished, Mom would pluck me out of the tub, wrap a fluffy towel around me and scoop me into her arms. Then she'd hug me real tight and spin me around, kissing my cheeks and laughing.

I don't know how much cleaning got done during those bath times, but I know I felt clean afterward. Clean and happy.

But the things I remember most about the baths were how Mom smiled at me. She had the prettiest eyes I'd ever seen. I remember standing in front of the mirror, staring at mine and wishing they'd get pretty.

Those are the fondest memories I have.

I climbed on the counter and stared into the mirror, looking at my eyes, wishing they'd turn blue, and pretty, like Mom's. My sister, Rachel, walked in.

"Hurry up, Sis. We'll be leaving in a minute."

"Where are we going?"

"To work with Mom. Like we do every day."

"I thought we were starting school."

"Not today," Rachel said. "Maybe next week. Besides, you're too young for school."

"Am not. Mom said I could go. Besides, I'm not staying with somebody again. Not ever."

"You'll stay wherever Mom tells you to stay. You're too little to argue."

"She said I'm going to school."

"She only said that because she's got nowhere else to put you. Why do you think she told you to lie about your birthday?"

"Just because you're in third grade doesn't make you smarter than me."

Rachel hugged me. "I didn't say I was smarter than you, but I've been around long enough to know about Mom, and why she does things." She rubbed my back. "You will, too. Pretty soon you will."

"What should I wear?"

"Jeans and sneakers. And don't forget a top. Mom will get pissed if you come out without a top."

"Don't worry. I'll be dressed," I said, and reached for a pair of jeans.

##

On the way to work, Mom said she would be stopping at the store on the way home. "Anything special you girls want?" she asked.

"Bananas!" we both hollered at once. We loved bananas.

"Anything else?" she asked. "It can't be much, but something little is okay."

"We're good," I said. "At least I am."

"Me too," my sister said, and we went back to playing "I Spy."

We played outside most of the day—and I dreamed of bananas—and when it was time to go home, Mom called from the street.

"Girls! Time to go."

We ran to the car and climbed in the back. "How did work go?" Rachel said.

"Just another day," Mom said. "Another day waiting for Mr. Right."

"Who is Mr. Right?" I asked, drawing a swift kick from Rachel.

Mom laughed. "He's the one who's going to take us away from all this," she said. "Give us a house and a home."

I grew excited. "When is this going to happen?"

She sighed. "As soon as I find him," Mom said, and then almost whispered, "As soon as I find him."

I reached into the bag of groceries on the back seat, looking for the bananas. When I didn't find them, panic set in. "Where are they?" I yelled. "Where are my bananas?"

I saw the expression on Mom's face in the mirror. "Oh God, dear. I forgot. I'm sorry. I'll get you some next time."

"Sure," I said, and curled my lip.

"Is that okay, honey? I just forgot."

"Sure, Mom," I said. But I noticed she hadn't forgotten his beer. It was in the bag. She wouldn't dare forget that.

##

Two weeks after that, Mom got a new job. "I got a raise," she said. "They're paying me two-hundred dollars more per month."

"That's great," Rachel said. "Now you can get that new dress you saw at the mall."

Mom sighed, then looked at us through the rearview mirror. "Who wants pizza?"

At first, I didn't believe what she asked. "Me," I yelled, and I figured she must have been telling the truth about the raise because we did get pizza that night. We never had money for pizza.

After pizza, we went home and played a few card games, and then we talked for a long time. Mom must have been happy because we never stayed up just to talk, at least not about nothing.

We talked for hours. It was late when we finally went to bed, but I couldn't sleep. I waited until Rachel's eyes were closed, and then I covered my head with the pillow and cried. Pretty soon, I felt Rachel move.

"What's wrong, Sis?"

"Nothing," I said.

"People don't cry over nothing."

"I'm just worried."

Rachel took the pillow off my head and turned me toward her.

"Why? Everything's going great."

I looked at Rachel and said, "I know, but that's what bothers me. Mom always says that whenever things are going too good, something bad is bound to happen."

"That's bullshit."

"You can't say words like that."

"I did, didn't I?"

"But you shouldn't. Mom said so."

"Go to sleep," Rachel said. "It's going to be a long day tomorrow."

I put the pillow over my head and scooted toward the edge of the bed. No matter what Rachel said, I knew something bad was going to happen. Knew it.

CHAPTER 2
THE PARK

The next day, we met Mom in the park after school. It was Wednesday, and she took off early from work to play with us—with us!

I was so excited. We went down the slide a million times, and we rode on a spinning platform, like a merry-go-round, and we played on the bars. We did everything.

I don't know how long we played that day, but it seemed like forever. I had so much fun, I didn't even mind the walk home or the fact that I had homework to do.

At dinner that night, I told Mom that I loved her, and I'd never be bad again. She laughed and just said, "We'll see."

When Mom tucked us in that night, we both told her how much fun we had with her. She smiled and said, "I'll make you a deal. If you are both good girls, and do your chores, I'll meet you every week after school, and we'll play, and that's a promise."

I couldn't believe my ears. Mom promised us, and she said promises were forever. She said that if you made someone a promise you had to keep it.

I knew I'd heard her right, but I wanted to make sure. I looked at Mom, staring at her beautiful smile. "Do you promise?" I asked.

Mom smiled, then she kissed me on the forehead, then she did the best thing ever—she crossed her heart and whispered, "I promise."

##

She kept that promise for three weeks. Then one day she didn't show up. After half an hour my sister said, "Let's go home."

But I said, "No way. She'll be here. She promised us."

"That doesn't matter," my sister said. "And we can't stay here all night."

"Just a little while," I said. "If she doesn't come in a little while, I'll go."

"All right," my sister said. "But only a little while."

I smiled. Mom would be here soon. She'd see. Mom made us a promise.

An hour later, we started walking home. Mom never showed.

Later that night, when I asked her about it, she said she got tied up at work and couldn't get away. She said it like it was nothing, and I didn't believe her.

It was like Rachel said: she just forgot us—like forgetting the bananas at the store.

Nothing was ever the same after that day. Don't get me wrong, we had some good days, but there were plenty of bad days, too. I didn't keep track, but if I had to guess, the bad days outnumbered the good.

Looking back on it, I guess the worst part about all this was the promise. Mom promised us she'd meet in the park, and she didn't. Just like the bananas, I thought.

CHAPTER 3
ON THE JOB

All the rookies were anxious about who they'd get for a partner, although at this point, partner meant a senior officer to watch over us for a few months. A mentor, partner, and guardian rolled into one. The senior officers were the ones that should have been nervous; they were taking on rookies.

Jason leaned toward me. "Who're you hoping for?"

"Doesn't much matter," I said.

"Don't give me that shit. I've seen you checking out Jefferson."

I wrinkled my brow and gave Jason a look. "Are you serious? He's old!"

Jason laughed. "He might be old, but he gets the ladies."

I shook my head. "You're all alike."

"And you love it," Jason said. "But don't worry, I've seen the way Jefferson looks at you, too. I'd bet fifty bucks he ends up your senior officer."

I laughed it off, but secretly hoped he was right. Jefferson was the one I wanted.

The first few pairings brought some much-needed laughter, especially when short little Margie got paired with six-foot eight-inches Kirkpatrick, and skin-and-bones Borsch got hooked up with a very-chunky Alicia Vick.

Jason jabbed me in the side when they called me to pair up with

Jefferson. I can't say I was disappointed. Everything else had gone according to plan, and it wouldn't be difficult to make this fit nicely with what I needed to do.

He walked over to me, boasting a swagger a lot of the younger cops had. His smile seemed genuine, but the look in his eyes matched the strut of his walk. The kind of look that had stripped me down already. I felt certain he was doing unimaginable things to my naked body in his mind.

"How do I look?" The words blurted out of my mouth before I realized how that sounded, but even that mishap went right for me.

It took him off guard. He lost his focus and stared, then mumbled, "I'm sorry?"

I flashed one of my disarming smiles. "I asked how I looked. I noticed you staring. Am I ready for the streets?"

That put him at ease. He returned my smile. "Ready? Yeah, I'd say you're ready. As long as you have a great partner." He reached out his hand to shake. "Senior Officer Jefferson," he said. "But everybody calls me Jeff."

"Rookie Lisa Benz," I said. "Everybody calls me Lisa." I laughed. "Great to be working together." Then I punched his arm and headed for the door. Now that I knew what worked, I intended to keep him unbalanced, despite his seniority.

We drew assignment in the Tenderloin District, and the first few days of patrol went as I anticipated.

##

We headed down Turk Street toward Taylor, going past the Tenderloin liquor store. There were already a couple of guys leaning against the wall, and it would be three hours before the store opened. Two more people were slumped over near the corner where Turk meets Taylor Street. One looked alive, but the other was questionable.

Jeff beeped the horn, then leaned toward me and hollered out the window.

"Show me you're alive," he said.

The one who looked questionable stirred at the sight of the cop car. He raised his arm and waved, and then laid his head against the wall. He shoved the guy next to him, who shoved back.

"Good enough for me," Jeff said.

"That's it? Show me you're alive?"

Jeff laughed. "If we got out to check on every drunk and drug addict that was slumped over against a building, we'd never get off Turk Street."

I sighed and then nodded. Some rookies got lucky on their first tour, got the areas where the cafés and coffee shops outnumbered the people. Jeff and I ended up in the Tenderloin, or Little Saigon as they called it now. Down here, the liquor stores and seedy hotels outnumbered everything except the drunks and drug addicts.

We rolled slowly past a grocery market that had metal bars on the windows. The sidewalk looked like it had been pissed on for a hundred years. I didn't get out to see if it smelled the same.

We went past the G&H liquor store on the corner of Jones, and past some apartments that didn't look horrible on the outside. A person might be fooled into thinking this wasn't a bad place if this was all they saw, but that perception wouldn't last longer than a few minutes.

Jeff took a right on Leavenworth and up to Eddy Street. Wasn't too much going on. A straggler here and there and everybody staring at us and then turning away. I felt certain we could've made our busts for the month if we checked everybody for half a dozen blocks, but Jeff seemed to be content cruising by, as if he had something else on his mind.

"Is this what it's going to be like? Cruising streets all day?"

"A lot of it," he said, "and when it isn't, you'll wish it was. Nights can be tough."

We passed a Vietnamese grocery store, and a shop that looked like it had nothing but porn videos, then Jeff went all the way up to Geary Street, where there were more clubs, more liquor stores, and then more liquor stores.

I stayed in the car as Jeff said, but I kept my eyes on him. He was talking to a couple of gangbangers—Asians, if my eyes weren't deceiving me—and they appeared agitated, hands waving, bodies postured for an argument or a fight. Jeff seemed at ease for a while, but then he grabbed one of them by the collar and yanked him close, using his left hand. His right went toward his gun.

I jumped out of the car and started toward them, but he waved me off. The gangbangers stepped back, relaxed. I stayed where I was, prepared to go in if necessary. Within a few minutes, Jeff returned.

"What the hell was that about?" I asked.

Jeff shrugged. "Couple of punks thinking they're tough."

"Do you know them?"

"Seen them around a few times. They're new here."

I got a bad feeling. Something was wrong. I didn't know what, but something. All my life I'd been able to tell when things were wrong. I still remember the first time it happened. That time is burned in my mind forever.

CHAPTER 4
SOMETHING IS WRONG

18 years ago, San Francisco

Rachel tapped my shoulder and whispered in my ear. "Time to get up, sleepy."

"What for?"

"First day of school, remember?"

I jumped out of bed and ran down the hall, laughing the whole way. "I get the bathroom first."

"You're a brat," Rachel said, but she didn't mean it.

I got dressed, then Rachel fixed me Cheerios and toast for breakfast. "What about lunch?" I said to Mom as she kissed me goodbye.

She knelt and put her arms around me, and then pulled Rachel into a three-way hug.

"Tell them you forgot to pack it," she said. "They won't let you go hungry."

"Won't they want money?"

Rachel patted my back. "Don't worry. I'll teach you how to do it. After a few days, they won't ask anymore." Then Rachel tugged my arm and said, "Hurry, or we'll be late."

"Bye, Mom," I said. "See you tonight."

She waved, and said, "Love you. Don't forget your age or your name."

As I walked to school, holding Rachel's hand, I felt like crying. It was my first day and I was going to have to tell two more lies.

Mom had prepared us well. Drilled us on our ages, new names, history, and everything else. All we needed to do was convince them we were real, and honest. The real part was easy. Honest was a different story.

A middle-aged woman stared at me from behind her desk. "Next," she said, and I stepped up before her.

"Name," she said.

"Marissa."

"Date of birth."

"October 11th, 1982." I had to lie. That's what Mom told me to do.

The woman looked me over. "Small for your age, aren't you?"

"Always have been," I said.

"Medical conditions?"

"None." I knew she shouldn't have asked, but I answered anyway.

"Did you fill out the form with address and contact information? If you didn't, it will be rejected."

"All done," I said.

"Have a seat to the right. Someone will show you where to go."

Ten minutes later, I was shown to Mrs. Buford's class. Buford looked like she had been there since about 1822. I'm sure it wasn't that long, but I didn't think it was far off.

I said goodbye to my sister, who was going by another name now. She had taken the name Rhonda because it started with an 'R,' just like Marissa and Morgan both began with 'M.'

Mom said it made it easier to make the transition that way, and I guess she was right; within a few weeks after using that name, I was answering when people called me 'Marissa,' although it took a lot of focus. I had, however, started calling Rachel by her new name of

Rhonda. The hardest part was when Mom called me Marissa. I missed my real name—if it was my real name.

"Good morning, Marissa. How are you this morning?"

"Fine," I said. She almost caught me by surprise calling me Marissa. Despite the practice I'd done with my sister, I wasn't naturally responding to the new name. Rhonda said it might take a little while longer.

I sat at a desk in the middle of the room, where I wouldn't attract much attention and opened up the reading book. I had no idea how to read, but I was a quick learner and figured it couldn't be too difficult.

Rachel, who now went by Rhonda, helped me with homework. Old Buford must have figured something was wrong when my homework was always right, and my classroom work wasn't, but if she suspected anything, she never mentioned it.

Two months went by and I was learning things. Buford turned out to be a good teacher, and she seemed to take an interest in me, helped me when I had trouble grasping new ideas. Once I started to get the hang of reading, the other subjects got easier: I could read the math problems, and I understood what English was about. It was getting to be fun.

One day, Rhonda was walking home with me, when someone called my name. Problem was, it was my old name.

"Morgan! Hey, Morgan." A girl ran across the street toward us. She was a second-grader and had lived near us before we moved.

I turned, instinctively, but caught myself and quickly turned back and ignored her.

She caught up to us within half a block. "Morgan," she said. "Remember me?"

I remembered her all right—1511 Dowd Street, Apartment C— but I wasn't about to tell her. Instead, I wrinkled my brow and said, "I don't know you, and besides, my name is Marissa."

She narrowed her eyes and stared. "Morgan, it's me, Janis. Remember?"

Rhonda, who was a fifth-grader, stepped up. She pointed her finger at Janis. "Listen, she already told you, her name is Marissa, so back off."

Now Janis looked confused. "I don't know what's going on here, but that's Morgan, and you're her big sister. That's all I know." She turned and walked back down the street, but kept looking back at us.

"What are we gonna do?" I asked.

"We're gonna tell Mom," Rhonda said. "She'll know what to do."

As we finished the walk home, I thought about what would happen. "Rhonda, I don't want to go anywhere else. I like it here, and Mrs. Buford is nice."

Rhonda walked for another ten steps or so. "We'll see what Mom says."

We were doing homework when Mom came home. "Hi, girls. How was school?"

"Somebody recognized Marissa," Rhonda said. "She lived in the building next to us on Dowd Street."

Mom began trembling and sweating. She looked as if she would fall. "Are you sure?"

"She came right up to us," Rhonda said. "No doubt about it. Knew me, too."

Mom paced in circles for a few seconds. "Start packing. We're leaving tomorrow."

"No!" I said. "I don't want to go."

"I don't care what you want," Mom said. "We're getting out of here tomorrow."

"But I like it here," I said.

"You'll like the next place just as much. Now help your sister pack."

"But why do we have to leave?" I asked.

"You remember Ted, and how he used to hit me?"

I lowered my head. "Yeah."

"We can't risk him finding us. So stop arguing, and get packing."

The next day we found an apartment in the Mission District. It wasn't a nice neighborhood, but it was a decent apartment. You could count the white families on one hand, including us; the rest were Mexican. It looked like we were going to have to learn Spanish to get along here.

Aside from the obvious negatives, there were positives, also. There were plenty of kids, and even though they spoke Spanish, they were friendly. It was warmer, too. Not as much wind or fog, though I didn't know why. And school was only three blocks away, a real nice benefit.

We registered for school the next morning and, of course, had new names. Mine was Manuela, and Rachel/Rhonda became Rosa. Mom said it would help us fit in if we used Spanish names. We changed our birthdates, too. Used the same days, just changed the month. Mine became March—like Manuela, they both started with 'ma'. And Rosa switched hers to October. It was the second letter of her new name, and it ended with 'r', the first letter. It made it easier to remember.

The morning went by slowly. I didn't know any of the kids in school, and they were all smarter than me. When the teacher asked questions about numbers or reading, most of the kids raised their hands. I slid lower in my seat so the teacher wouldn't see me.

I knew it was only a few hours before the bell rang for lunch, but it felt like forever. I rushed to the hallway and got second in line. The teacher marched us toward the cafeteria, but it was at a very slow pace. I wanted to run because I couldn't wait to see Rachel.

We went down two long halls, and then turned left into a huge room with lots of tables. I poked my head to the side, looking all over, holding my breath. Then I heard her voice.

"Little sister," Rachel—Rosa—said.

I breathed easier. Rosa was my best friend.

She came over, took me by the hand, and said, "Hi, Mrs. Gibson."

The teacher looked at her, then me. "Rosa, so good to see you."

"This is my sister," Rosa said. "Can she sit at the table with me?"

"Of course, she can," Mrs. Gibson said.

She took us aside and whispered, "Rosa, do you girls have lunch?"

"Not today," Rosa said, "but that's okay, we're not—"

"Nonsense. Let me get the class seated and I'll take care of it."

When Mrs. Gibson left, Rosa poked my arm. "See, it's easy. You'll get used to it."

I nodded and smiled. I wouldn't tell Rosa, but I didn't want to get used to it.

At the end of the day, Rosa was waiting for me outside the classroom.

"You have a good day?" she asked.

"It was okay," I said, but once we were alone, I told her I was scared.

"That's okay. I was too for the first week or so. It gets easier after that."

"Where are we going?" I asked.

"Mom said to meet her at the playground on the way home. She'll be there in about an hour."

Rosa and I had so much fun that I lost track of time. She was pushing me on the swing when I heard Mom's voice.

"Are you girls having fun?"

I jumped off in midair and ran to her. "Mom!"

"How was your first day at school?" she asked.

"It was good," I said. "Will you stay and play with us?"

She tilted her head like she was going to say no but she surprised me with a smile and said, "Okay, for a little while."

She pushed me on the swing, rode down the slide with me, and we even climbed the monkey bars together. Then Mom said she was worn out and went to sit on the bench. Rosa and I kept playing.

We had so much fun that day that Mom decided to meet us once a week. So every Wednesday she'd come to the playground around four o'clock and we'd be a family. We did this for six months, never missing a week. It didn't matter that we had no money and lived in a terrible place, or that I had to lie to get lunch from the school. Those six months were the happiest times of my life. It all changed in early March.

Mom met us like usual, and we played, like usual. Then she went to sit on the bench. I was in the sandbox with Rosa, building tunnels.

The next time I looked over, a man was sitting next to her on the bench. They were talking.

"Who's that?" I asked.

"Never saw him," Rosa said.

I got out of the sandbox. "What's Mom doing talking to him? She said never talk to strangers."

"That rule is only for kids," Rosa said.

Mom kept talking to him, and I didn't like it. After a long time, I grabbed Rosa and said, "Let's get Mom. I want to go home."

Mom stood and pulled me toward her when I got close to her, but she didn't say anything, almost like she was embarrassed by us.

I looked up at the man. "Who are you?"

Mom squeezed my arm and started to say something, but the man interrupted her.

"That's all right," he said, and then he leaned down next to me.

"My name's Marc, and I'm a friend of your mother's."

He smiled, but it wasn't a real smile. "What's your name?"

"Little sister," I said, and Rosa laughed.

"Tell him your name," Mom said.

He pretended to laugh, and then he stood. "That's all right. I have to be going anyway." He looked at Mom and said, "We're good for Tuesday, then?"

"Tuesday's great," Mom said. "See you then."

All the way home, Mom kept telling us how wonderful Marc was, and that he might be the man she was waiting for. When we got to a busy corner, she got close to us and said, "In every girl's life, there is a man who is meant to love her forever—unconditionally. Some women don't ever find that man, which means somewhere out there a lonely man is looking for his special partner. But the lucky girls find their loves. And if you find your special love, it's better than anything."

I didn't say anything to Mom. I didn't even talk to Rosa about it, because she was just like Mom. But I knew that Marc wasn't going to be that man. I knew.

The big night was finally close, and Mom was more nervous than I'd ever seen her. She was determined to make a good impression on this guy, so she wanted us to clean the apartment, and clean it nice.

Our apartment was so small the three of us could clean it in two hours. Mom had us working for two days before Marc came over.

"I want it spotless," she said. "Men don't like a dirty house."

I wondered why she cared more about what Marc liked than what Rosa and I liked, but I didn't say anything.

Marc brought her flowers that night, and he brought Rosa and me stuffed bears. Mom cooked a meatloaf, and he told her how good it was. I didn't know what the big deal was—it was a plain old meatloaf, and Mom wasn't the best cook.

He came by once a week, normally on Friday nights, but after the first few visits, he stopped bringing things for us. And after a few more, he stopped bringing them for Mom, too. The only thing he brought now was beer.

Mom used to laugh at the silly things we did. Now he'd raise his eyebrows and look at her, and she'd holler at us, or send us to our room. That was a joke, too. Our room was a tiny little space he walled off from Mom's bedroom. All we had was a single bed and some hooks on the wall to hang our clothes, and two blankets draped over an opening to make a doorway. I didn't mind not having any room, but we could hear everything that went on in Mom's room. That's what I didn't like. Sometimes I heard her cry.

He was always gone when I woke up for school, and we wouldn't hear from him again until Friday night when he'd stop by with his beer. He never seemed to get drunk, but he did enjoy drinking.

The next few weeks at school turned out to be good. Señora Cortes was our new teacher, and she proved to be very nice, even nicer than Buford. Some of the kids didn't speak English, so she asked us to teach them. It felt good. While we taught them English, they taught us Spanish, and that helped us get along better.

The first few months went fine. At school, we were learning, and making new friends, and things at home were good. Then one night Mom brought Marc home again. She came in the door with a box of pizza. She knew we loved pizza, so I guess she thought she'd bribe us with it.

"You remember Marc," she said, and they sat at the table. Marc had a friendly smile, and Mom seemed to like him enough; in fact, she said he was great. And she sure saw him enough.

We ate dinner and talked, and then we played a game of Uno. Rachel/Rhonda/Rosa—whoever she wanted to be called—won. Afterward, Marc and Mom drank a few beers, then he left. Later that night, Mom gave us a bath and tucked us in.

"Remember I told you about Mr. Right, and how he would come along someday and take care of us? Well, I think Marc could be him. He's sweet, handsome, has a good job, and, most importantly, likes you girls. I want you both to try hard to make him feel at home. Okay?"

"Sure, Mom," Rosa said, and I nodded.

Mom kissed us goodnight and smiled as she turned up the blankets. After Mom left the room, Rosa leaned over and asked, "What do you think?"

"You mean about Mr. Right?"

"Yeah."

"All of our lives, Mom has been telling us about Mr. Right, and how he would come along some day and take us out of poverty and into a nice house with a swimming pool. We'd all have nice clothes and money to spend."

"So, what's wrong with that?" Rosa asked.

"Nothing's wrong," I said. "If he's Mr. Right. But as far as I'm concerned, something about Mr. Right is wrong."

CHAPTER 5
A SHINY NEW BADGE

San Francisco, present day.

We started out the day the same as always, patrolling the streets in the Tenderloin, but something was different today. Jeff wasn't taking his time. He did everything in a hurry. Before I knew it, we were heading up Geary Street.

I was focused on an apparent junkie near the corner coffee shop, when I noticed Jeff looking at me. "You look familiar," he said. "Something about the way your profile is…" The statement caught me by surprise, but I recovered quickly. "I hope so. I asked you enough questions when you came to the academy training class."

Jeff shot me a puzzled look.

"Remember? You were guest-teaching and had an open-questions session? I was the one in the back with all the questions."

"Oh, yeah," he said, but I could tell he didn't remember. Probably because it didn't happen, but he would never know that.

Five minutes later, he pulled to the curb across from the coffee shop where the junkie had been and got out. "You want anything?"

I shook my head. "Already had two coffees," I said. "I'm good." This had become a routine: stopping at the shop for coffee and Jeff asking if I wanted any. I never did, but he asked anyway.

The first few weeks on patrol went as expected—driving the Tenderloin District, with its seemingly endless array of bars and sleazy motels, handing out too many tickets, making small talk with the bums—oh, and dodging passes by Senior Officer Asshole.

Did this son of a bitch really think I was going to fall for his lines? Did he go home dreaming of plopping me down naked in bed somewhere? If he did, then this guy didn't know who he'd partnered with. What he needed was a reality check.

On day eight, as we were driving down Geary Street, Jeff got a text on his cell. He glanced at it, then dialed a number.

"Where are you?" Jeff said.

I heard the guy on the other end say something but couldn't make it out, then Jeff responded. "I'm not far from there. Give me ten minutes."

"What was that about?"

"Might have a lead on something."

"What?"

"Don't know yet. We're heading there now."

"Heading where?"

"Down Geary, by Larkin. Some ramshackle motel."

"In that section of the city there are entire blocks consisting of nothing but ramshackle motels."

"Not if you count the dive bars and drug dealers," Jeff said. "If there are ramshackle motels, then there are dive bars and if there are dive bars, then there are drug dealers."

About ten minutes later, we pulled to the curb at the corner of Larkin and Geary. It was a seedy neighborhood, full of run-down apartments with balconies ready to fall off, and motels begging for customers that stayed longer than an hour, and didn't leave used condoms on the floor. The apartment windows that weren't broken were open, with T-shirts, socks, and underwear drooping from clotheslines attached to rusted eye hooks hammered into crumbling mortar joints of old brick walls.

"Stay in the car," he said as he opened the door.

"What's going on?"

"I need to see a guy. He gets nervous if anyone else is there." He smiled, the kind of smile he gave when he lied. I'd made that *tell* already. I didn't know what he was up to, but I went along with it.

"How long are you going to be?" I asked.

"Not long. Hang tight."

He walked into a building that looked as if it should have been condemned. An alley separated it from another building that looked even worse, and from the smell of it, there could have been anything underneath the garbage, piled knee deep in some areas. I left the car running and stood outside, leaning against the car. The exhaust fumes were bad, but at least they covered up the stench from the alley.

Three young Asians—who looked to be gangbangers—approached from the south side of the street. Their eyes were on me and I didn't like the looks on their faces. I kept my eyes open, shifting them from one spot to another, checking for suspicious activity. This was the kind of situation they told us about in training. The kind that could get you killed if you weren't careful.

The gangbangers started across the street, not looking to see if there were cars. They had the *feel* of the neighborhood, knowing it was safe to cross. I recognized it because I had it where I grew up, if you want to call it that.

I straightened, got balanced, planted my feet, and unbuckled my gun, keeping my hand close. They were close enough now that I could see their tats—gang members for sure. From where I stood, they looked to be Vietnamese, and, considering the neighborhood, that fit. After all, what *did* you expect to find in Little Saigon?

The guy in the middle slowed, held his hand out to the others, and fixed me with a glare. "Relax, Rook. Just passing through."

I nodded and tried to remain calm. "No worries."

They walked by, but kept an eye on my gun hand. It wasn't until they passed that I realized they had been as nervous and scared as I was. *Welcome to the streets, Rookie.*

I could sense if someone was behind me, on the side of me, if they were watching my ass, or waiting for me to make a bad move so they could mug me. It was the kind of sense that had saved me a hundred times when I was growing up, and I was counting on it a few more times.

Jeff's "not long" time frame turned out to be 30 minutes. He came out shaking his head like nothing panned out, but he shot looks up and down the street as if someone might be watching. That attitude made me suspect otherwise.

"What was that about?" I asked as he walked toward the car.

"Nothing," he said. "Just a guy I had to talk to."

"Talk about what?" I said, not giving up as easily as I'm sure he hoped I would.

"Nothing important," he said. "Now, if you're done with the third-degree questioning, let me drive."

On the way home, Jeff was chatty, even more than normal. I wasn't paying attention. I was busy thinking about what happened earlier, when those gang bangers were on the street. I was scared, no doubt. But I had been ready to draw my weapon and fire. One wrong move and I'd have popped one or more of them.

Maybe the guys at the academy were right. Maybe I *was* destined to kill someone my first year.

CHAPTER 6
SOMETHING *WAS* WRONG

San Francisco, 15 years ago.

We were walking to school, passing the corner drug store, where a homeless guy was sleeping in the doorway. "He was gone again this morning," I said.

"Who?"

"Marc. Who do you think?" I said.

"What time did you get up?"

"You know I can't tell time, but it was still dark."

We were about halfway down the block when I reached over and tugged on Rosa's sleeve. "Where do you think he goes when he's not at our apartment?"

Rosa said, "I think he's married."

"Why do you think that?"

"Just do. That's all."

"Do all men do that?"

Rosa shrugged. "Tina's mom says so."

"I wish Mom would find somebody else," I said.

"Me too," said Rosa.

"I thought you liked him?" I said.

"I did at first, but now I don't. I don't even know if Mom likes him now."

"Why do you say that?"

"I heard them fighting the other night, and Mom said she wished she never met him, then he got mad and threw an empty beer can at her."

"I'm glad it wasn't a bottle," I said.

"Yeah," Rosa said. "If he had a bottle, he'd have probably thrown it."

Three months passed, and Mom was still seeing Marc. Despite that, things were good. Mom and Marc were getting along—except when Mom cried. I heard her crying one night and got out of bed to see what was going on, but Rosa stopped me.

"Don't. There's nothing we can do. Not now. Not yet."

"What do you mean?"

"I mean we're not old enough to interfere—yet. Someday we will be, though."

Rosa was usually right, so I listened to her and went back to bed. For several nights, there was a lot of fighting, but after a few weeks, things got better again.

On a nice day, in late May, we met Mom at the park as usual, then we walked home. Marc was waiting at the door for us. He had some Chinese take-out in his hands.

"What took you so long?" he asked.

"Nothing," Mom said. "We were playing at the park."

"And leaving my ass out in the cold."

"I wouldn't do that. I didn't know you were here."

"And would you have been here if you *had* known?"

"The thing is, I *didn't* know. That's the end of it."

"It's not even close to the end of it. You left me here to freeze my ass off while you played with the girls. Make sure that doesn't happen again."

Mom gave him one of her 'don't start this' looks, and opened the door to go inside.

Despite the welcome addition of the take-out food, the dinner table was tense—few conversations—and afterward, Rosa and I took a quick bath before climbing into bed for the night.

A loud noise woke me around ten-thirty. It was arguing and it was coming from Mom's room. I whispered to Rosa, but she was sound asleep. I got out of bed and crept down the hall to see what was going on.

Mom and Marc were yelling, but I couldn't hear what they were saying. As I got closer, the voices became clearer. Mom was telling Marc that she wouldn't put up with it. He said he could look at anyone he wanted to.

It wasn't long before I realized he was talking about Rosa, that *she* was the one he was staring at. *How disgusting!* Rosa was pretty, but it was disgusting that he was thinking of her like that.

I listened a while longer, then sneaked back to my room. I lay in bed trying to decide whether to tell Rosa or not, but by the time I finally fell asleep—hours later—I still hadn't made up my mind. I was scared, and I wondered why Mom was even with Marc, let alone living with him. *Why couldn't she see that he was an asshole? Why did she always pick guys like that—like Ted and Phil?*

Six months later, Marc hit Mom for the first time, or at least the first time that I knew about it. Mom had a black eye and bruised face when I saw her at breakfast. She said it was an accident, but Rosa and I didn't believe it, and Mom knew we didn't. About a month later, Marc beat her again, but this time it was far worse. She needed to get stitches above her left eye.

We moved out after that. Packed everything we could in the car and headed out to find a new apartment—and a new school to go to. Mom drove to the other side of town and we checked into a motel, the kind where you can pay cash and no questions are asked.

We unloaded the stuff from the car, and then we drove to a used car dealer and Mom sold her car. We walked back to the motel.

"How're you gonna get to work?" I asked.

"I'm getting a new job," she said, and the way she said it told me it was the end of the conversation. I took the hint and didn't ask any more questions.

Everything changed from that day on. We stayed for a month in the motel, moved to another one for a month or so, and after that we found a run-down apartment to rent. It was bigger than our old one, but it was really dirty and in a bad area. Rosa and I hadn't been to school since this happened. I know most kids would like that. I did too, for a week or so, but after that, I missed it. I wanted kids to play with. And as weird as it sounds, I wanted to learn.

Rosa kept asking Mom what happened, and what we were going to do. At first, Mom ignored her, but one night she sat with us after dinner and told us.

"Marc was a bad man," she said. "You know he beat me. But he would have done worse. If I hadn't left, he would have hurt you girls." She hugged us tight. "I could never let him do that."

"We'll be okay," Rosa said.

"Yeah, Mom. We'll be fine," I said.

Mom shook her head. "Don't *ever* think that. He can find us anywhere. That's why I'm using a different name, and why you can't go to school."

"For how long?" I asked.

"We'll have to see," she said. "It'll be a while. Maybe next year."

For the next six months, I got my wish about learning. I learned how to run, how to steal, how to lie, and when none of that worked, I learned how to fight. People think only boys have to fight to survive, but where we lived, everybody had to fight. Didn't matter if you were a boy, girl, or a dog. If you wanted to live, you fought.

Mom was miserable, then the inevitable happened—she told us to pack for another move. She said she thought Marc might have found us.

This move wasn't as bad as the others, because, for once, we all wanted to go. I didn't like Marc, and neither did Rosa. "Didn't trust him" was probably a better way to say it. There were times when he seemed creepy.

Mom had never noticed, but maybe now she did. I hoped so, anyway. We needed to get away from him.

This time we ended up by North Beach, the old Italian section of the city. Some of the old people still spoke Italian, but the younger ones were Americanized, and spoke English. Despite that, we changed names. Mine became Marcella and my sister became Rosanna. We would fit right in.

The first night, Mom ordered from a local restaurant called "The Stinking Rose," located on Columbus, just north of Broadway. It was a famous tourist trap that used garlic on everything, even ice cream. Some people loved it, others hated it. I know the aroma was addictive. Just get within a block and you wanted to go eat, at least I did.

Mom and I split the Spinach Fontina Fondue, and it was delicious. It was so good, that I swore if we ate there again, that's what I'll get for the main meal. Rosanna had the pizza, but she didn't like it. She thought it had too much garlic on it; if I had ordered the pizza, it wouldn't have been a problem because I loved garlic. Mom liked her meal, but said she had eaten at a similar restaurant in L.A.—also called The Stinking Rose—and swore it was better.

I didn't put much faith in what she said because, to Mom, everything was rated by how good a time she had. If she enjoyed herself and the company was good, then she would swear the food was great. On the other hand, if she had a bad time, then the food rating would suffer. Of course, I guess we were all like that, to some extent.

When we finally settled in, we ended up going to Garfield Elementary School, on Filbert Street. It turned out to be a good school, with a well-deserved reputation. We lived at some apartment on Union Street, so it wasn't much of a walk to get to school, but the streets were steep, even for San Francisco. The street where we lived was steep enough that the cars had to park sideways instead of straight with the curb. It made walking a daily chore. I don't know how Mom afforded the place, but I wasn't complaining.

Rosa, or Rosanna, as she was now known by, had grown into a young lady, and she was gorgeous! Maybe all the walking on those steep streets had toned her legs. All of the boys wanted to date her, and as I later found out, they wanted to do more than date.

We had lived there for more than a couple of years now, and I had made friends. I was also used to my new name, which was now Maddy. It might have been the longest amount of time I had ever been called by the same name.

We missed the whole first year of school, but started back in August. Mom went through the routine of telling us how to lie to get food, but she didn't have to. Rosanna and I had grown into expert liars. We knew when to lower our heads, when to pout, when to look up at people with sorrowful puppy-dog eyes, and most important of all, we knew when to make our voices crack, as if tears were bursting to get out.

It always took me a few weeks to get used to the names, especially the first name, but I understood why Mom had us change them. If somebody was looking for you, and they were smart, they'd know that people usually keep the same first name. Mom said it was better if we got used to changing it. Rachel and I practiced by calling each other by name every time we spoke, so instead of, "Hey, what're you doing?" I'd say, "Hey, Rosanna, what're you doing?"

She'd respond by saying, "I'm fine, Maddy."

The other thing we did was give each other nicknames. She

became Big Sis and I was Little Sis. Mom said we could keep nicknames, even when we changed regular names. It made it easier all the way around.

As we got ready for school, Mom gave us a crash course on remembering our birthdays and on how to get a free lunch. "Most important of all," she said, "is to remember your new names. This is crucial. Don't *ever* tell anyone your old names. *Ever.*"

Mom finished drinking her coffee, and talked about saving enough money to move out and find someplace nice to live, a place where she could get a good job, and maybe even save for a house.

Two years later, we were still in that rat-infested apartment. At first, I didn't notice, but the longer we lived there, the more I realized it was not the place I thought it had been.

The only good thing about living there was that no one would think to look for us—not in that dump. The neighborhood was mostly drug addicts and dealers, mixed in with people worse off than us.

Despite our circumstances, things were starting to get better. Mom wasn't as nervous as she used to be and Rosanna was doing great in school. I was still behind the rest of the class, but one of the teachers volunteered to help me and I was starting to catch up. We even had some nights at home where we laughed like we used to.

Christmas was three weeks away. I went to bed dreaming of what Mom always told us, that someday a nice man would find us and take care of us, and things would be great.

Two days before Christmas, he found us. But it *wasn't* the nice man.

PREMONITIONS

Jeff met me at the station in the morning. We chatted it up with a few other cops, then got in the car and hit the streets. As we drove down Eddy Street, Jeff slowed and pulled over to the curb. It was time for morning coffee, and nothing interfered with that, except a homicide. I grabbed an outside table while he got coffee. A few minutes later, he returned with two coffees and sat next to me.

"What's on the agenda?" I asked.

He took a bite of a cinnamon twist, took a slow sip of coffee, and said, "Nothing different. Cruise the streets. Talk to some folks. Find out what's going on."

"What about yesterday?"

"What about it?"

"Come on, you know what I'm talkin' about, and I'm your goddamn partner."

"If it was important, I'd let you know," he said. "Trust is the number one issue with partners."

I took that to mean I wasn't going to be let in on whatever the hell was going on, so I didn't push.

***

The day started out same as all of them did, cruising the streets, stopping to talk with shop owners, keeping a close eye on potential trouble. Three kids made a quick turn as we approached the corner.

Jeff pulled over and got out. Before he could tell me to stay inside, I got out too.

"What's the rush?" he said.

They looked to be Asian, Vietnamese if I had to guess. I didn't see any tats, so no gang affiliations.

The one closest to us turned toward Jeff and said, "No rush. Just time to leave."

"Just stay a while," Jeff said. "And put your hands on the wall."

"What you breakin' our chops for?" This from the only one to speak so far.

"Just checking to see what you're carrying," Jeff said.

I unbuckled my gun, just to be safe, and kept an eye on the other two.

"Ain't carrying nothin'."

"Then this won't take long," Jeff said.

The one with the mouth said, "Don't do this shit at the Metropolis."

Jeff shot me a look, then spun the kid around. "What the hell's that supposed to mean?"

"Shut up, dude."

I glared at the kid who said it. "Your turn to shut up."

Jeff had the mouth with his back to the wall, facing him. "What about the Metropolis?"

He shook his head. "Didn't mean nothin'. Just talking."

Jeff reached into the kid's pocket and pulled out a small bag. It looked to have a few pills in it.

"What the fuck? That shit ain't mine."

"It goes away if what you tell me sounds good," Jeff said.

I looked to the kid, then Jeff, while trying to keep my eyes on the other two. I couldn't tell if Jeff had anything in his hands when he reached in, but I didn't think so. Besides, he was my partner.

Jeff let the kids go, but he put the pills in his pocket. We got in the car and pulled away from the curb.

"What are we doin' with the pills?" I asked.

"Don't worry about it. I'll take care of it."

I didn't say anything more, but after driving around for half an hour, I said, "Were they yours?"

Jeff looked over, eyes narrowed. "What?"

"The pills. Did the kid really have them?"

"Officer Benz, I don't know what the hell they're teaching at the Academy nowadays, but whatever they told you about crooked cops, you are *not* partnered with one." He flashed a thin smile. "And for the record, the pills belonged to the *kid*, and we *are* turning them in. If you're wondering why I didn't bust him, it's because this lead might turn into something better. Besides, we can always get those kids later. If they're messing with pills they're not stopping because of what happened today."

"Okay, but I had to ask."

We turned on Mason, drove for a while, then ended up back on Eddy. It wasn't even noon and I had already seen more than my share of drunks, junkies, and transvestites than anyone should have to. Throw in the whores, derelicts and drug dealers and I'd had my fill for the whole damn week.

We cruised for another half an hour and then Jeff spotted another coffee shop, prompting an urge. While he went for drinks, I spotted suspicious activity on the corner.

Five kids were hanging by the light pole across the street. They looked like ordinary gangbangers, dressed in tattered jeans and short leather jackets. Four of them were definitely Asian. Since we were in Little Saigon, I assumed they were Vietnamese, same as the others we had run across. The Vietnamese had been good for the neighborhood—in general—but like most immigrants, they came with their own baggage, and that baggage was in the form of the AZN Boyz.

I got out of the car and approached them, after unbuckling my gun holster. One of them looked my way, then said, "What's goin' on?"

"That's what I'm here to find out," I said. "Gathering pretty early, aren't you?"

"I could say it's none of your business," he said.

"And I could say, turn around and put your hands on the wall. All of you."

"What for? We ain't done nothing wrong."

"I'll decide that after I search you."

"We got rights," he said.

"Those rights went away a long time ago," I said. "Now, do what I said."

A few minutes later, Jeff walked across the street, holding two cups of coffee. He set them on the hood of the car, and drew his gun. "Any problems?" he asked.

"None I can't handle," I said. "Couple of punks breaking bad's all."

That remark drew a sneer from a few of them.

"We takin' them in, or lettin' them go?" Jeff asked.

I thought for a few seconds. We had nothing to hold them on. "I guess we're letting them go—for now."

The leader of the group smirked, which made me want to lock him up right then. "See you around, bitch," he said. Then they all walked away.

We got back into the car and continued driving.

"Be careful," Jeff said. "They have no respect, and if one of them had been carrying heavy weight, and they suspected you were about to take them down, they wouldn't have hesitated to kill you, no matter the heat it would bring." He paused to signal a left turn, then looked back at me.

"This is the Tenderloin, and it's no place to mess around. The people here don't care if they go to jail. All it means is that they're served three meals a day, and they get to spend time with family and friends. They plain don't care, so be careful."

"I'll be careful, but I'm not looking the other way."

Three days later, during another coffee-shop stop, I noticed the same gangbangers huddling together on the same corner. I got out of the car and approached. Before I knew it, they formed a circle around me, and began crowding my space.

"Take it easy," I said.

"We'll take it easy when you stop givin' us shit," one of them said, and he moved even closer.

I was about to call for help, when I heard Jeff's voice. "Hands against the wall, fuckers. Don't make any sudden moves or I'll plant you deep."

The guys moved toward the wall. A quick search revealed a small amount of heroin in one of their pockets. After that, Jeff had them in cuffs. He put two of them in the back seat of our car, and called another patrol car to get the other three.

On the way to the station, the skinny, long-haired one said, "What do we need to do to get this to go away?"

"What have you got in mind?" Jeff asked.

"Shut-up!" the heavier, clean-cut one said.

"I ain't doin' hard time," second one says. "Besides, it was a bad bust. That bitch planted the drugs on us."

A smile lit the heavier one's face. "Had to be. We didn't have no drugs."

Jeff looked at me, pulled to the curb and then got out. He signaled me to join him.

"Is that right—what he's sayin'? Did you plant the drugs?"

"What difference does it make? You *know* they do drugs."

"Planting drugs went out with the '60s."

"You're dreaming."

"Is that what they teach in the academy now?" Jeff asked.

"Now I know you're dreaming. Planting drugs is still as alive as prostitution or wife beating. Nothing went out with the '60s, except maybe your memory."

He shook his head and headed back toward the car. "Follow my lead," he said, and opened the door.

"What have you got to trade?" Jeff said, and stared at the skinny one.

"Don't say a fuckin' word," the other one said.

"Fuck that," the first one said, then he turned his head toward Jeff.

"I know a guard at San Quentin that runs China White, and a lot of it. It's a big operation. I mean a *big* one."

The heavy gangbanger grabbed the other one by the hair and yanked him to the side. He butted his head. "Shut the fuck up! You know what'll happen."

Blood gushed from both of their foreheads. "I don't care what happens. I'll leave. Go south. But I ain't goin' to prison."

"You pussy bitch. What would your brother say?"

"Wouldn't say shit, because he's sittin' on death row. Not me, motherfucker. Ain't catchin' me waitin' for no needle."

"Needle's already got your name on it, bitch. You're just too stupid to see it."

Jeff stared over the seat at them. "Tell me what you know. If it's big enough, this bust might go away."

"Fuck you. This is goin' away, regardless. That bitch planted drugs on us."

The skinny one spoke up next. "Guard up at San Quentin's runnin' tar and whores both. Makes a delivery about every week."

Jeff pointed at the heavy guy. "Shut the fuck up." Then he turned to the other one and said, "What's the angle?"

"Passes off the whores as wives lookin' for 'booty call' visits. Tar is straight up."

"Who pays for the booty calls?" Jeff asked.

"Poor guys can't pay because they got no money. Rich guys don't need to pay because they're so rich their wives will wait, regardless. That leaves the middle-classers. Got enough money to pay for ass, but not enough to convince the wives to wait."

"What about the tar?"

"Guard's got an inside man who splits it up into eight-balls and then sells the eight-balls to guys who split it up more. Profits are huge."

Jeff sighed. "I imagine they are. After a few months in prison, a man will pay anything for a real piece of ass." He looked back at the guy we had nicknamed 'Skinny' and said, "Tell me how this works. Who's the supplier? When do they meet and where?"

"That'd be easy," Skinny said. "We supply the bitches and my brother's boys supply the dope."

Jeff nodded and then smiled. "You just might come out of this with more than a walk."

"That's what I'm lookin' for," Skinny said. "Gonna walk all the way to L.A."

"L.A.'s not big enough to hide your ass. We find you no matter what."

"'We find you.' You mean *we'll* find you, don't you? It looks like you lost your grammar lessons. Besides, L.A.'s a big place. There are plenty of spots to hide," Skinny said.

"Plenty of AZN Boyz down there, too, and each one's got two eyes. You're a dead motherfucker."

"The meet's set up for Thursday night," Skinny said. "Gonna' be at 7:00 at the Phoenix, on Eddy Street. Room 112."

"You'll have to bust me, too, so he doesn't suspect anything. And make it look real."

"No need to worry about that," Jeff said. "It'll look real enough."

"What about the drugs?" I asked.

"Saturday. Same place. Same room."

"Okay, get out of here before somebody sees you," Jeff said. Then he pointed his finger at me. "And Lisa will be one of the 'girls' you introduce. Don't worry. She can handle it."

Skinny and his buddy got out of the car and headed down the street. I looked at Jeff with a blank stare. "'She can handle it?' What the hell was that all about? I've never done UC work."

"It's about time you started," Jeff said.

"What the hell do you have in mind?" I asked.

"Pass you off as one of the whores, get them to pick up the drugs, then bust them for all of it."

"Aren't you turning this into the boss?"

"We're doing this ourselves. It will look good."

"It'll look good if I don't get killed. Or didn't you think about that? Or don't you care?"

"I thought about it, and I *do* care, but I'm confident you can hold your end."

I thought about Jeff's proposition, and how it would look on my record, then said, "Let's do it." But I wasn't nearly as confident as Jeff.

CHAPTER 7
A NIGHT AT HOME

Not long after my thirteenth birthday, Mom took us to the mall so we could shop for each other. It was getting close to Christmas, so she gave Rosanna and me five dollars each and said, "Use it to buy a present for each other. I'll wait in the food court."

We decided to spend the money on Mom instead of ourselves. With ten dollars, we could get her something nice. Besides, we didn't need anything.

It only took us half an hour to shop. We got her a bottle of a special bath soap she liked, one she hadn't bought since we lived at the old apartment. We even had it gift wrapped, then went back to meet her. As we crossed the food court, I could see that Mom was sitting at a table with somebody. His back was facing us. "Who's that?" I asked.

Rosanna slowed down. She grabbed hold of my arm and held me back. "Hang on, Little Sister."

We were about twenty feet away from them when he turned around. I stopped dead. Rosanna moved toward Mom. "Are you all right?" she said.

Mom was shaking. "I'm fine."

I could tell by her voice she wasn't.

Marc had moved toward us. He was close enough to grab us. "Hello, girls. It's been a long time."

"Not long enough," I said.

He laughed. "I'm sure you don't mean that," he said.

"I mean it, all right," I said. "We don't like you."

"That's funny," Marc said. "Your mother invited me to dinner this weekend."

I almost fell over. *How could she? Why* would *she?*

"I'll bring pizza," he said.

He must have thought pizza would take the sting out, but it didn't. It somehow hurt more.

He and Mom talked for about fifteen more minutes, then he left, saying he'd see us this weekend.

"You didn't tell him where we lived, did you?" I asked Mom.

"He said he'd help us get a new apartment," Mom said.

"You know he's lying," Rosanna said. "He just wants to get back in your life."

"Nonsense. You have to have some trust."

"That's not how you taught me," Rosanna said. "You taught me to suspect everyone's motivations."

"That only applies to strangers," Mom said.

"As far as I'm concerned, he's a stranger to us," I said.

"I know it seems that way," Mom said, "but he's a nice man."

Rosanna quit arguing. I grunted. When Mom made up her mind, there wasn't much we could do about it. I kept quiet, and dreaded the night he'd come over.

I didn't have to dread for long. Marc stopped by that weekend, and he brought an ample supply of beer, enough to keep him drunk from Friday till Sunday. To top it off, he surprised me by spending the night with us, something he hadn't done much.

Rosanna and I went to bed around 9:00. Sometime around midnight, I heard noises from Mom's room. I went to see what was going on. As I crept closer, I could hear Marc's raised voice, and

Mom was yelling even louder.

"Don't you ever…" Mom said.

"I'll do what I want," Marc said.

The next thing I heard was the sound of a slap. Then the sound of a lamp hitting the floor. Then Marc yelling, "You son of a bitch."

I went back to my room to tell Rosanna. She would know what to do.

"Get out!" Rosanna said. "Now!"

"Where?"

"Anywhere. Go to the cops, or the hospital. Just get out of here. I don't trust him."

"What about you?" I said, then we heard Mom scream.

Rosanna shouted, "Run! Don't tell *anyone* your name, not even the cops."

"Come on," I said, but she wouldn't leave.

Rosanna ran down the hall to Mom's room. I wanted to follow her, but I wanted to leave, too. I didn't know what to do.

Finally, I decided to sneak down the hall and see what was going on. The closer I got, the clearer I could hear Rosanna scream. Mom was quiet.

When I pushed the door open, he was standing there with his pants down. Rosanna was on the bed—her clothes were off—and Mom was on the floor, bleeding.

I grabbed the scissors off the nightstand and stabbed him in the back, then I ran down the hall and locked the door.

Within five minutes, the door burst open, and Marc ran in. He grabbed me and threw me on the bed, then he started ripping my clothes off. I was able to break free, then screamed and jumped from the bed. I ran behind him, and pushed on the scissors, still sticking out of his back

He hollered and reached around to yank out the scissors.

I ran for the window and opened it, then climbed on the sill. It looked like a million miles to the ground, but I knew it was only about twelve feet. Still, that seemed like a long way, and I was little.

I thought about it, then thought more. I kept thinking about it until I heard Marc's voice as he came across the room.

"Let's see who runs this house," he said.

I jumped before he finished talking, then I heard Rosanna scream again as I hit the ground. I hid in the bushes, then, when I felt it was safe, I made a run for it. I ran for three blocks before I found a phone I could use. I dialed 9-1-1.

"9-1-1. What is your emergency?"

"Somebody's hurting my mom and sister," I said. "Hurry. We live on Union, at the corner of Kearney."

I hung up the phone, and hid in an empty doorway until the ambulance came. Before long, they came out of the house with three gurneys. One was covered with sheets. My chest tightened. *Who was under the sheets?*

After a few minutes, the ambulance left, sirens blaring, and thirty seconds later a cop car came. I was tempted to go talk to them, tell them what happened, but then I remembered what Mom and Rosanna said about not trusting anyone, not even the cops, so I stayed hidden and waited for them to leave.

A few days later, I found out they took Mom and Rosanna to St. Francis Hospital on Hyde Street. It wasn't far away, so I decided to sneak in and see them.

The hospital sat on Hyde, between Pine and Bush. I waited for a middle-aged couple to walk in and followed them. Anyone who looked would think I was with them. At the first split in the hallway, I turned right and went on my own, looking for a nurses' station. I didn't have to go far. Two nurses were at the desk.

"What room is Rosanna Mercaldo in?" I asked.

The nurse stared at me. "Who are you?" she asked.

"Maddy. Her sister," I said.

She smiled, then searched the computer. "She's in room 212."

"And my mother?" I asked.

She hesitated, then said, "I'm sure the doctor will talk to you while you're visiting your sister."

"Okay, thanks," I said, and left to find the elevator.

When I got to room 212, Rosanna was sleeping, but a doctor was there. "Where's my mom?" I asked.

He sat in one of the chairs, and said, "Your mother suffered serious injuries."

"What kind of injuries?"

He held my hand and said, "I'm sorry, Maddy, but your mother didn't make it. She died."

"What! How? Why?"

"Someone hurt her, and the internal bleeding killed her. I know the police are looking into it."

"No!" I screamed. "She couldn't have died. She couldn't have."

The doctor pulled me to him and hugged me. "It will be all right," he said. "We'll find you some place to stay."

"Okay," I said, through tears, then—when he let go—I ran from the room and out of the hospital. On this day, my life changed forever.

That's when I found out Mom was dead. That's when I learned that Marc wasn't even arrested. That's when I swore to kill Marc. *He'd pay for what he did.*

CHAPTER 8
ON THE RUN

Tears poured down my face as I left the hospital. *What would I do now? What* could *I do? I had nowhere to go and no one to live with.* As I walked out the front door, a cop car was pulling to the curb.

"There she is," one of them yelled, and pointed at me.

I ran as fast as I could, and I kept running. After five or six blocks, my lungs felt as if they were on fire. My chest hurt, and I couldn't breathe right. Halfway up the hill, I stopped, hands resting on my knees as I gasped for air. I looked behind me for the hundredth time in the past few minutes. No one. Nothing but fog. Thank God for that. I let a little hope fill me.

Maybe I'd ditched them. Maybe I'd really gotten away. All that was good, but where the hell could I go? I had no family. No friends. No one. And it was now clear I couldn't trust the cops, just like Mom said.

All the running made me hungry. And thirsty. I walked a few more blocks, constantly checking to see if I'd been followed.

Up ahead was a recessed doorway. An old homeless man was curled up against the wall, his head resting on a stack of newspapers and his body covered with a coat for a blanket. I looked behind me again, and then ducked into the doorway.

He didn't stir. I moved closer, sat on the concrete walk with my knees raised and my back propped against the wall. I glanced at the man again. He wasn't as old as I thought. Just dirty. I wondered why he was homeless, and then it hit me. I was homeless too.

I was homeless, and I was starving.

And freezing, I thought, and moved even closer to the homeless guy, trying to get some of his warmth. I *almost* wanted to crawl in under his coat, but there was no way I was getting that close.

The first night on the street was more than frightening. It seemed as if every time I closed my eyes, the wind howled louder down the funnels carved from the skyscrapers. If I blinked too often to clear my eyes, the sounds of people walking and talking, murmuring about whispers of plots—maybe to kill me—kept me wide awake. At one point, I looked at a clock in a store window. It was 3:45, and I cried. I couldn't imagine falling asleep anytime soon and I needed rest.

At about 4:40, the homeless guy—who I now knew to be called Mick—woke up and looked at me. "You okay, girl? Looks like you've been crying."

I sobbed, and nodded. "I've got nothing left. I never had much, but now I lost my mother and my sister. What am I gonna do?"

Mick moved close and put his arm on my shoulder. His sleeve was covered with dirt from the sidewalk, and his unshaven face held a layer or two of grime. "It's not easy, girl. Startin' over is never easy, but when ya' got nothin' to start with, it makes it harder. Some say it makes it easier because you've got nothin' to decide on—no other place to start—and they might be right about that. But hard or easy, either way, you're gonna do it."

He pulled me close and let my head rest on his shoulder.

"You can do it. I see the strength in you. You'll make it if you want to." He gave me a squeeze and a pat on the back. "You'll make it even if you don't want to."

Sometime before morning, I fell asleep. I jumped when I felt someone shaking me. My eyes popped open, early morning sunlight catching me by surprise. I poked my head out of the recess and looked down the street both ways.

"Whoever you're running from ain't here," Mick said.

I looked at him. No question he was homeless, but under all the grime he looked…clean. His smile showed all his teeth, and his eyes showed his smile. "Who said I'm running?"

Mick laughed. "Seen enough young girls in trouble to know. But you're the youngest. Want to tell me what happened and who's after you?"

I glanced at Mick, then back down the street. My stomach growled, but felt sick at the same time. I shook my head.

"Run away from home?" he asked.

Another shake of the head.

He looked me over. "Can't imagine anyone tossing out such a cute little thing as you. You got parents?"

The "cute little thing" comment almost scared me, but then I realized he said it with warmth, not in a creepy way.

I looked down at my shoes, filthy from running the streets, and took a deep breath. "My mom's dead. I never had a dad."

"I'm sorry to hear that," he said, and I believed him. He sounded sorry.

I looked up at him, trying not to cry, but I couldn't help it.

When the tears came, he pulled me to him and hugged me. It didn't matter that he was dirty, or that he stunk—he was somebody who cared about me, and right now I needed that more than anything.

As I lay against his chest, he rocked back and forth. "When did she die?"

My crying turned to sobs. "Last night."

He held me tighter. "My God. You poor girl."

After a minute or so, he stood, taking me by the hand. "They'll be here to roust us pretty soon. Let's find something to eat."

"I'm starved," I said.

"Me too," he said. And then, "You're gonna need a coat. Nights get cold out here. But I guess you know that now."

My arms were wrapped around my body, trying to stay warm. "Mornings are pretty cold, too," I said.

"What's your name?" he asked.

I almost told him, but then shook my head. "My mom said never trust anyone."

"Your mom was a smart woman. But that's all right. You probably need a new name anyway."

We walked a few blocks and he said, "How about Millicent for a name? We could call you Millie."

"We'll see," I said, but a few blocks later, I ditched him. Mom had told me never to trust anyone, and I learned that in spades with Marc. I knew it would be tough fending for myself, but I was determined to try it.

I slept on the streets that night, in the doorway of a jewelry store. The owner woke me the next morning, and not in a nice, gentle manner.

"Get up, bitch," he said. "I don't want no junkies hanging around here."

I saw no sense in telling him I was just a scared, hungry, young kid. I don't think he'd have cared, so I simply left, muttering an unkind thought or two along the way.

I hadn't gone three blocks when I ran into a few kids about my age, or a little older.

"What's up?" one of them said. He was the cutest in the bunch.

"Nothin'," I said. "Just lookin' for a place to stay."

"How old are you?"

"Fourteen."

"Got the place to stay," he said. "Come with us."

I followed them for a few blocks. When he turned to enter an abandoned building, I hesitated.

"Where are you going?" I asked.

"Just follow us," he said. "You can stay here."

"What's it gonna cost?" I asked. "I don't have any money."

"We'll work something out," the good-looking one said.

"I don't want to 'work something out,'" I said. "I want to know now."

"No big deal," the guy said. "You take your clothes off and do us all, and you can stay here."

"No way!" I said. "You're nuts." I turned to leave. He grabbed my arm, but I broke free and ran. Halfway down the block, I looked behind me. They were chasing me, so I kicked it into another gear. I turned the corner and headed up the hill, hoping they'd get out of breath. I was almost up the first block, when an older guy stopped me. It was Mick.

"Where you goin', Millie? What's your hurry?"

It looked like I was gettin' that name whether I liked it or not. "Some kids chasing me," I said.

"What are they chasing you for?" he asked.

I looked down the street. They were still coming, so I turned to go. The old man grabbed me by the arm. "Stay here," he said.

He walked toward the kids, who stopped when they saw him.

"Hey, Mick," one of them said.

"Hey," said the others.

"What are you boys after?" Mick asked.

"Nothin'," they said at once.

"That's a lie!" I yelled. "They tried to screw me."

"Is that true?" Mick asked.

"Just wanted some payment for room and board," the cute one—who I didn't think was cute anymore—said.

"And where do *you* send your room-and-board checks?" Mick asked.

"You know we don't pay no room and board," one of them answered.

"But you want it from her?"

"I guess."

"Tell you what," Mick said. "From now on, pretend that this girl is my daughter. Treat her like that and we'll be okay. Treat her any other way, and I'll be visiting you." Mick shot them a hard glare. "Understand?"

"Yeah," they all said, then turned to leave.

I looked up at Mick in a new light. He was unkempt, with a scraggly beard, but he had a friendly look on his face, and a soft, warm voice, just like I remembered. Despite what Mom had said, maybe he was someone I *could* trust.

"Thanks," I said.

"No need for thanks," he said. "I was just doing the right thing for you."

"Not many people would have done that," I said.

"More than you think, girl. The problem is that not many people would put themselves in a position to do it. If they did, they'd have done it."

I thought about what he said, and had to agree. "I guess so."

"So what are you gonna do now? You got a place to stay?" he asked.

"Not yet."

"I stay down by Union Square, where you were last night. You're welcome to hang out there, if you want."

It didn't take me long to make up my mind. "Fine by me. Lead the way, 'cause I forgot."

He started walking, then took me by the hand. "First thing we gotta do is get you a blanket," he said. "Nights can get damn cold."

"I found that out last night, but I don't have any money," I said.

"Don't worry about money. I know a place where they give out blankets for free to anyone who needs it."

"Where?"

"Down on 6th Street. It's not far. Maybe a twenty-five minute walk. Then it's only another twenty minutes to home."

I stopped. "What do they want for the blanket?"

"I told you. It's free. Some people do things for others. Not everybody wants to screw you."

"Those boys wanted to screw me," I said.

He laughed. "That they did. And can't say I blame them; you're a pretty girl. I imagine if I were young again, I'd want to screw you, too, so don't blame them. Besides, it's a fact of life—young healthy boys want to screw young pretty girls. End of story."

At first, I was angry, then I thought about what he said and realized he was probably right. After that, I continued along with him.

We walked to 6th Street and got a blanket, then we headed back to Union Square. It didn't take us long to get there; Mick walked fast for an old man, and he knew all the shortcuts. Just after dark, we settled into a cozy corner of one of the stores by the coffee shop. I pulled the blanket over my shoulders and tried to sleep. It's not that I didn't trust Mick, because I'd made up my mind to give him a chance, but at this stage of the game, I couldn't afford to trust anyone.

Before long, I fell asleep, and didn't wake until I heard Mick's voice.

"Time to get up, girl. They'll be here to roust us soon, and we don't want to give them cause to toss us out of here. If we don't cause trouble, they won't bother us."

"What kind of trouble?" I asked.

"Bein' here when customers show up. Gettin' in the way of the people who work here. Things like that. Stay out of their way and they won't bother you."

"Makes sense," I said. "So, how do we stay out of their way?"

"Get up early. Clean up. Don't beg from the customers. That's probably the most important rule; they hate it when you mess with the customers."

"Where do you beg?"

"Not where you sleep. You've heard the saying, 'don't shit where you eat.' Well, 'don't beg where you sleep' is even more important for people like us."

We went a lot of places that day. He got me a coat and a few clothes and an old sack to carry them in.

"The sack has to look dirty," he said. "If it's new, somebody's gonna steal it from you. And while they're stealing, they might do more.

"What's your name again?" Mick asked.

"Can't tell you," I said. "It's not safe. He'll get me."

"Don't worry about it. You'll be safe."

"I'll make up a new name. I've been living with new names all my life."

Mick stared with a sensitive look. "Here's the plan. I'll take you to the center and tell them I found you wandering the streets."

"No way."

"All you have to do is say that you don't remember anything, not even your name. They won't have any way to find out—unless your fingerprints are on file."

"But what if they—"

He shook his head. "If you keep telling them you don't remember, soon they'll stop trying."

"What good will it do? Going into a home, I mean."

"They'll find people who want you. People who will care for you, and keep you fed and clothed. They'll make sure you go to school. And take you to the doctor when you're sick." He turned me to face him and looked into my eyes. "You can't ask for more than that. Not in this life."

I lasted six months in the center—until the assistant director noticed me 'blossoming,' and decided I should have company when I slept. I left the next day and found Mick.

"Didn't work out," I said. "Had the same problem as before. Seems like everyone wants to screw you—literally."

Mick nodded. "That *is* a problem." He spread out a blanket and patted it. "You can stay here," he said. "Nobody will bother you."

Pretty soon, Mick taught me the ins and outs of the streets—how to beg, how to steal purses, and what kind of scams worked on what kind of people. He also taught me about daytime gangs, and nighttime gangs. During the day, the pickpockets, purse snatchers, and hard core beggars were prevalent, but at night—that's when the real gangs roamed.

They took down anyone for anything. The only things they cared about were the cops, and they didn't care much about them. So, when the sun went down, Mick made sure we were tucked away safely. It wasn't just the gangs either, but the cold. San Francisco got damn cold at night—even in the summer.

About one month later, the cops came looking for me, asking everyone if they'd seen me. Fortunately, this wasn't a law-abiding group, so the cops received no cooperation. Mick questioned me that night.

"What did you do? Cops are looking everywhere for you."

I shrugged.

He got a hard look to him, one I'd never seen before. "If I'm going to protect you and risk my ass, you need to be straight with me."

I sat silent.

"Still waiting," he said, and his look hadn't changed.

I thought about what Mom said, but figured Mick deserved some trust.

"I might have killed a guy," I said.

"*Might have?* Might have is an odd way to put it when you're talkin' about a killin'."

"I'm not sure if I did or not."

"Why don't you tell me about it?"

I thought about what Mick asked, and decided I had to trust somebody, sometime. "My mom was seeing a guy named Marc. He was an asshole and I'm pretty sure he was married. I wouldn't have minded that as much, but he treated my mom and my sister like shit."

"Tell me how," Mick said.

I felt my disgust curl my lips. "He beat my mom. And he…"

Mick waited.

"And he raped my sister. Turns out he killed my mom, so I killed him, or I think I did."

"How did you kill him?"

"He was doing that to my sister, so I stabbed him in the back with a big pair of scissors."

"In the back? You sure you killed him?"

"I'm not sure, but I saw the ambulance carry him out, like they did my mom."

"What about your sister? Where's she?"

"I don't know. When they stop lookin' for me, I'm gonna have to find her."

Mick rubbed my hair and held me close. "I know you won't like this suggestion, but you should let me take you to the cops. They can't blame you for what you did. If you just tell them—"

I pulled back. "No way! I'm not trusting anybody."

Mick patted my back and rubbed it. "Okay. Don't worry. You can stay right here, but if you're gonna stay, we have to teach you," Mick said.

Before long, I was earning twice as much as he was. No surprise. A nice, young girl on the streets was bound to get more 'tips' than an old guy.

Mick had good advice, though.

"Always smile," he said. "People will give money to you a lot more often if you're smiling. And always thank them. Also, try to remember who gave you what. If someone gives you a dollar, and you thank them the next week and tell them how much it meant to you, you're more likely to get more. You might get two dollars the next time. Hell, you might even get five."

Mick was right. I got to know all of my "customers," even the ones who only gave a quarter. In three months, I was bringing in more than fifty dollars a day, almost three times what Mick brought in.

Mick had contacts at a few restaurants and hotels where we got scraps and leftovers, so we never had to worry about food. Sometimes, we'd get a dish where the patron wasn't hungry, or didn't like what they ordered, and we'd have a feast.

At other times, there was next to nothing, and we'd have to combine it with others. On rare occasions, we'd go hungry.

With the money I was bringing in, we could afford to splurge. Once a month, we got a loaf of bread from the bakery. On those days, we stuffed. Coffee was another luxury. Mick had an array of customers at the coffee shop, so we were never in need of a good cup of coffee, even if it was only half a cup at times.

One night—a holiday—we retired early and talked. I asked Mick what he was doing out there.

"Lost my job," he said. "Then I lost my wife and my house. Next I knew, I was out here begging. My daughter wasn't much older than you when this happened." He looked the other way. "Sure do miss her."

Then he turned to me. "How about you?"

"Just lookin' to kill a man—if he's not dead," I said, and for the thousandth time, I thought about what I'd do to Marc when I found him.

CHAPTER 9
LIFE ON THE STREETS

Mick wasn't a typical homeless man. He didn't drink and he didn't do drugs. Besides that, he was damn smart. Not only did he know about everything there was to know on the streets, he knew about book smarts, too.

Every night he'd teach me: reading, math, finance, all of it—even history. By the end of the second year, I was probably ahead of the kids at school.

Things were going fine on the streets. Mick protected me, and made sure I was fed and clothed, although I brought in most of the money now.

Mom had long ago passed away, and Rosanna wasn't getting any better. I hadn't gone to visit, but Mick knew a guy who worked in the kitchen, and he checked in on her.

I had taken on the name Millicent, as suggested. Mick and everyone else called me Millie, and as far as anyone but Mick knew, *that* was my name.

One day, Mick asked me to run an errand for him to the Tenderloin. It was only a ten-minute walk from Union Square. It's not like anyone would want to go to the TL, but if they did, it wasn't far.

I headed out around ten o'clock and figured I'd be back by eleven. Near the Uptown Market, at the corner of Ellis and Larkin, a group of Asian gangbangers were hanging out.

Three of them stepped in front of me, blocking the way.

"Please move," I said.

One of the guys, dressed in tight pants and wearing a cheap leather jacket with obnoxious zippers, said, "Binh, she wants us to move."

The one who appeared to be the leader of the group stepped forward. "We're not moving. Ain't happening."

"Fine," I said, "then I'll go around you," I moved toward the curb.

Two of the gang members blocked my way, and Binh said, "You're not going anywhere, bitch."

"Great, then you can buy me a cup of coffee," I said with bravado, though I was scared to death.

Binh laughed. "Girl's got balls, I'll say that. Where you get them?"

"The guy I live with—Mick."

A frightened look came over all their faces. Binh said, "You live with Mick, up on the Square?"

"Have been for a few years," I said.

He eyed me up and down. "Damn! Got more respect for the Mick now than I did before." He signaled to the rest of them, then stepped aside. "I'm gonna check this out. If you're lyin', you're in shit. If you're bein' straight, you're welcome here any time. In fact, you'll be safe anywhere down here."

I nodded. "I'm not lyin'," I said, and went on my way.

The respect they showed Mick got me curious, and I found out he had killed a few people who were messin' with him. Seemed like Mick knew his shit from his time in the service and he wasn't afraid to use it.

Anyway, it wasn't long before the word got out. "Millie" was under Mick's protection. Also, "Millie" was under the protection of the AZN Boyz. The gang consisted of Chinese and Vietnamese members, mostly younger ones, and they were fierce rivals with the Wah Ching, a more organized, older gang.

Knowing Binh and his friends were in the AZN made me even more curious. *Why did they care about what Mick thought? Why would a tough street gang give a shit about a homeless man?* Then I found out that two of the guys Mick killed were in the Wah Ching, and he had killed them for messing with the AZN.

I told Mick about the situation later that night, and I asked him about it. He said he'd tell me sometime. One week later, I woke up and found a knife in his chest. He was dead. I could only assume the Wah Ching had caught up with him.

I found Binh and Duong hanging out at a coffee shop early in the afternoon. "Did you kill Mick?" I asked, knowing my tone was demanding, but I needed to verify my suspicions about the Wah Ching.

The news shocked him. "Not only did I *not* kill him, I'm going to find out who did," he said, and he and Duong left the shop and turned to go up the street.

It didn't take Binh long to get the information. A guy named Tran, who ran a bookie joint on Larkin, had him killed. Seems like he owed Mick a lot of money.

"Don't worry," Binh said. "I'll get revenge, and I'll get the money, too."

True to his word, Binh found me one week later—after Mick's funeral—and handed me an envelope bulging with cash. "Here's what Tran owed Mick," he said. "And by the way, Tran is dead. Fell out a window."

I nodded, then said, "Thanks. I thought it was the Wah Ching."

"Me too," Binh said. "Which is why I went lookin'. Needed to settle scores no matter who it was." He gave me a sideways glance.

"You got a place to stay?" Binh asked.

I thought for a moment, then said, "Not permanent. They kicked me out of where we were, because of Mick gettin' killed. I've got to find a new place."

"We've got an extra room," Binh said. "You can use it if you want. No foolin' around required."

I liked what he said, and I believed him. Besides, it would be nice to be recognized as truly under their protection. "Deal," I said. "I'll move in this week."

I was still mourning Mick's death, but I found time to pack the few things I had and head down to Binh's apartment. That night, I went to bed and felt safe for the first time in many years.

I pulled out the letter Mick had written me. The cops had given it to me at the funeral, but I hadn't found the courage to open it yet.

> *Dear Millie:*
>
> *You have been like the daughter that left me. I haven't seen her in years, so your company has been more than appreciated.*
>
> *There were many things I did that I shouldn't have, but I did them for her. Every penny I made from illegal operations, I deposited in an account for her, hoping for a reconciliation. Now, I know that won't happen, so I want you to have it. Do something good with it. Get off the streets, and find your dreams.*
>
> *Love,*
> *Mick*

Inside the envelope was a statement from the bank. He had $472 thousand dollars in the banking account. "What the hell?" I said. "Where did he get this?" It made me wonder why he lived on the streets.

I turned to Binh. "Where did he get this? And why was he on the streets?"

"He got the money from his work," Binh said. He had been watching from the doorway. "He told me he was going to give it to you, in case you didn't get the letter." Binh smiled. "Mick was a good guy. Gave me my start when I was about ten."

Binh sat on the edge of my bed. "Mick was a complex guy. He could have lived a normal life with the money he had, but he chose to stay on the streets. Maybe he got used to it like guys get used to prison. Who knows?"

He surprised me by what he said. I sat there thinking about how this would affect my life.

"Take the money and get out," Binh said. "He left you enough to get a great start. Don't hang around like Mick did."

"What about you?" I said.

"I don't need anything," Binh said. "I like it here, and I like what I'm doing." He paused for a minute, then pushed my leg aside. "Go on. Get out."

I thought about what Binh said. The money would definitely set me up in something, but what. The only thing I knew I wanted to do was kill some guy named Marc. And I intended to get it done.

CHAPTER 10
A DEATH IN THE CITY

Eight years ago, San Francisco.

It was only six o'clock and it was already dark, a sure sign of winter. A biting cold rode in with the night, and it stung like someone slapping my face. I wrapped a scarf tighter around my neck, and took another sip of coffee. The temperature must have dropped ten degrees in the last hour. With the wind picking up, it felt more like twenty.

Binh came up behind me, blowing hot breath into his hands. "Cold."

"You don't have to say it. Anyone who's outside knows it." I took another sip of coffee, and offered some to Binh. He grabbed the cup and took a swig, ignoring the steam rising from the cup.

"Did you decide what you're doin' with Mick's money yet?"

I looked at Binh, wondering if he had an ulterior motive for asking. Though I had no reason to suspect that he did, Mick had taught me to be suspicious of everyone. "Not yet, but I'm working on it."

He handed me a slip of paper with a name written on it. "Phuc Nguyen is a financial wizard," Binh said. "I already spoke to him. If you want help, he'll fix you up. He can figure out the tax problems also."

I tucked the paper in my pocket, and thanked Binh for the help. "You're a good man, Binh."

"I keep telling people that, but there are some who would argue with you," he said.

I laughed. "I guess they just don't know you."

I met Phuc the next week to discuss my situation.

"You're a wealthy girl now," Phuc said. "It's time to start a new life. You have enough money to buy a house and get off the streets, and you'll have enough left over to keep you going for at least a few years. Depending on the type of job you have, maybe longer. If you find a decent job and are frugal, this money will probably last ten years."

"And then what?" I asked.

"By then, you'll likely be married, or you should be, as good as you look."

"Who the hell wants to be married," I said.

Phuc looked at me strangely. "It can be good. All you need is the proper arrangement. Find an older gentleman with a full bank account, and marry for the money. This city is not short of older, rich men wanting sweet, young girls like you to show off. Find the right one and you don't even have to sleep with him. Find the 'really' right one and you can sleep with whomever you want—no repercussions."

I smiled. "Let me know when you find that guy. I just might go for an arrangement like that."

Phuc made a note in his book. "I will," he said. "That might not be as difficult as you think."

Phuc kissed me on the cheek, and walked out the door. I had a suspicion that the man he was talking about might be himself, but I wondered why.

I started thinking about how I was going to manage my new life. One thing for sure—if I intended to live a respectable life, I needed a new identity and it had to be a good one. *Maybe Binh could help with that.*

##

I found Binh hanging on the corner of Larkin and Eddy, the heart of Little Saigon. "I need advice, Binh, and I'm willing to pay for it."

"Forget the pay. What do you need?"

"A new identity," I said. "And not some shabby piece of shit, like you guys use. I need a *real* identity and a damn good one."

He thought for a minute, then said, "What you need is a dead body where nobody knows she's dead. Maybe a young hooker. Something like that."

"And where the hell do I get one?"

"Leave that to me," Binh said.

"Whoa! I don't want you killing anybody."

"Don't worry. I won't kill anyone for you, but I might steal a body—enough of them around. What we need is the right one. I'll put the word out."

"I'd owe you big time if you deliver."

"You already owe me big time," Binh said. "I do this, and you'll owe me more."

##

Three months rolled by, and there was still no stiff from Binh. I stopped by his corner one day. "What's the word? I need to get movin'."

"You'll get movin' when we have a decent body," Binh said, "unless you want to gain a few hundred pounds or magically become black. Do that, and I'll fix you up."

I laughed, but was crying on the inside. I was tired of living on the streets. When it was a daily routine, I hadn't thought much about it, but now that I had some money it was a different story.

Two weeks later, Phuc got hold of me. "Remember that special arrangement I told you about?" he said. "I know someone who's interested."

"What's the catch?" I asked. "Is the guy gay? Is that why he doesn't care if I fool around?"

"Does it make a difference?" Phuc asked.

"Is the guy you?" I said.

"Does *that* make a difference?"

I thought about what Mick taught me. "It does, and I'll have to say, 'no thanks.' Mick told me that anyone who made his money with money can't be trusted in real-life decisions. He said they'd always be deciding on the side of the finance."

"But this is—"

"Gotta pass," I said, "but thanks."

"You still want me to handle your money?" Phuc asked.

"If you don't have a problem with it, I don't have a problem. You've already done a great job. Might as well keep going. We can both make a lot of money."

Phuc laughed. "That's what we'll do then."

Phuc had me invest my money in biotech and technology companies. Fortunately, one of them was Apple.

Soon, I became wealthy beyond my wildest dreams. I didn't have to worry about money anymore, at least not compared to how I was living.

Fifteen months went by without a match on a body. I slept with a knife gripped in my hand every night, ready to use it if necessary. I guess I never realized how much comfort Mick had provided.

One night, I heard a noise, like someone sneaking up on me. I held the handle of the blade tightly, focused, and tried to see who it was. It was Binh, and he had a girl who appeared to be drunk leaning on his shoulder

"Give me a hand, goddamnit."

I let go of the knife, and reached up to grab hold of her. As soon as I touched her, I knew she was dead. "What the hell? Did you kill her?"

"No, but I might have found you a name to wear."

I was trying to contain my excitement, and all the while, a flood of questions ran through me. "What about her license? Her fingerprints? Her —"

Binh said, "As far as I know, she's never been busted, so fingerprints shouldn't be a problem. And I *know* she's not old enough to drive, so she's got no license. I think you'll be pretty safe with her."

"What about the body?" I said.

"Without ID, it'll just be another body takin' up space in the morgue. They won't keep it long."

Binh handed me an ID card for the library, something more than a few homeless did to have a place to hang out. Her picture was on the front of the card.

"Look at the bright side," Binh said. "She's a fresh kill, and she looks enough like you that you could pass for her. If anyone asks, just explain that when this picture was taken, you were on drugs, and now you're straight. That will explain a lot."

"What about people looking for her?" I asked.

"Won't happen," Binh said. "She was a junkie whore. No family. No friends."

"So what do I do?"

He pointed to the ID card with her picture. "We'll have to get this fixed up, but after that, you'll be fine. As I said, she doesn't have a license, and there's no need to worry about fingerprints."

"What about cops?" I asked.

"If she's wanted for something bad, 'fess up and tell them you stole her identity from her dead body. Anything else, take the bust and move on."

I nodded. "What's her name?" I asked.

"Lisa," he said. "Lisa Benz."

CHAPTER 11
WHERE IS ROSANNA?

Now that I had enough money to make a difference, I knew what I had to do—find Rosanna. She had been hospitalized since the night Mom died, and I *had* to find out how she was, as she had been moved to another hospital.

I asked Binh for help, and even offered him money for his services. He was insulted at the offer of money, but he did help.

Within two weeks he located Rosanna—she was at St. Mary's, over by Fulton and Stanyan. I guess they must have moved her there.

The next day I went to visit. I asked for Rosanna Mercaldo, and was shown to her room, but when I walked in, she was just lying there—in a coma.

Her eyes were closed and she couldn't move, couldn't even talk. "Rosanna," I said. "It's me. Rosanna, do you hear me?"

Whether she heard or not, I didn't know. Regardless, I was heartbroken. There lay my sister, the only one I could share memories with, and she couldn't even talk to me.

After about twenty minutes, the doctor walked in. I spoke to her, but she said there wasn't much hope; in fact, she said that if nothing changed—either in Rosanna's condition or finances—she probably was not long for this world.

Panicked, I instructed the doctor to give Rosanna the best care she could and I would foot the bills. Before I left, I filled out a few forms and left a P.O. box as the address to send the bills and any correspondence.

I stayed for another hour, sitting by her side, reading her books, telling her stories. It didn't matter that she wouldn't—or probably couldn't—hear; I told them anyway. I cried as I talked of the times we used to play jacks or when we'd meet Mom at the park. It was painful to see her there, in this condition. I wished there was something I could do.

I leaned over, kissed Rosanna goodbye, and made her a promise that I would get the guy who did this to her. I'd find out if he was alive, and if he was, he would not live another year—not after what he did to her and Mom.

Before I had come into her room, I was questioning my mission in life; now my resolve was steeled. *Marc*—if he wasn't dead—was going to die.

This was a promise I intended to keep.

CHAPTER 12
AN OFF-THE-BOOKS STING

We set up the deal with Skinny. I was going to be one of four girls he supplied to the dirty guard.

I met him at 6:00 on Thursday, and we went over the plan. Skinny would "introduce" us, then the guard would tell us when and where to meet so he could escort us to the prison.

At 6:50, we were in front of the Phoenix Hotel, four girls and Skinny. We made our way to room 112, where we met Roger, the guard from San Quentin.

He eyed us carefully, then said to me, "You don't look like no whore."

"That's because I'm not," I said. "My husband is doing ten years down in Avenol. I don't get to see him, but I still need lovin'."

Roger ran his stare up and down my body, then smiled. "They're gonna love you," he said. "Not often they get a taste of real meat."

"Just remember that when it's time to pay," I said.

"Your pay is the same," Roger said.

"The same? Filet mignon costs more than flank steak," I said.

Roger smiled. "Show what you're worth, then we'll discuss it."

"Deal," I said.

A few minutes later, Jeff walked in, dressed in the finest threads, looking like a street thug.

"Lookin' for Roger," he said.

"Who's lookin' and what for?" Roger asked.

"Your new supplier," Jeff said. "Hong Le is dead."

"Regardless of whether he is, or isn't, what makes you think I would want you as a supplier of whatever it is you believe I need?"

"Because I used to supply Hong Le. There is no sense in paying profit for a middle man. If you buy direct from me, you'll save money."

"And what would be the cost?"

"I can save you ten grand off what you were paying, and give you the same shit."

"I've only got one problem with that," Roger said. "Hong Le might not like the change in business."

"Like I said earlier, Hong Le is dead."

A man stepped out from behind the door. "Hong Le is *not* dead," he said. "But you will soon be."

Jeff pulled out a gun and shot him twice in the chest. He turned to Roger. "As I said, Hong Le is dead. Now can we do business?"

"I don't see why not," Roger said.

I stared at Hong Le's body, lying on the floor, blood pooling under him. I couldn't believe Jeff shot him! *What the hell was going on? What did I get myself into?*

I sat silent during the price negotiations. Before long, Jeff left. A few minutes later, Roger told me to meet him next Friday, at 8:00 in the morning.

"We'll get there early," he said. "Plenty of time to enjoy the day."

I left a minute later, along with the other girls, and walked down the street. Skinny waited on the corner.

"I heard there was some trouble," he said.

"Trouble? What trouble?" I wasn't about to let him know what happened, despite my misgiving.

"I heard Hong Le got shot."

"Shot? I didn't see anything."

"Didn't see anything, huh? I guess your partner didn't either." He gave me a skeptical look, then said, "Just make sure you show up when Roger told you to. He gets pissed if you're late."

"Don't worry. I'll be there on time."

We walked three blocks to a little restaurant and had some Vietnamese noodle soup. I had crackers and coffee with mine. Twenty minutes later, when we felt it was safe, Jeff showed up.

"You okay?" he asked.

"I'm okay," I said. What I wanted to say was, "I can't say the same about Hong Le." But since Skinny was still with us, I held my tongue.

"Hurry up and finish the soup," Jeff said. "We have a lot of work to do."

It took me ten more minutes to finish eating, then we left and headed for Jeff's car. He had switched with the patrol car at the station, so we wouldn't be made by Roger, or anyone else.

We were riding up California Street, when I turned to Jeff. "We should give this to the boss."

"Not going to happen."

"We've already got one person dead. What are you waiting for?"

"I'm waiting to bust this fucker. It's a big enough deal that it might earn me a promotion. Look good for you, too."

"On the other hand, if they find out about Hong Le, we'd both be busted."

"No way they'll find out."

"You think Roger won't run his mouth? That's a laugh," I said. "At the first sign of a deal, he'll tell everything he knows."

"Roger won't tell anything," Jeff said. "Trust me."

"That kind of talk scares me, Jeff."

"You'll get over it," Jeff said. "Now, shut up while I think this through."

I didn't like his tone, but I wasn't about to argue with him, especially after seeing what he did to Hong Le, so I shut my mouth, closed my eyes, and tried to enjoy the ride.

I would have enjoyed the ride a lot more if I hadn't just seen the guy next to me kill a man. Of course, knowing that man was a scumbag drug dealer helped soften the blow.

"Are you ready for Friday?" Jeff asked.

"As ready as I'll ever be."

"This is dangerous, and don't let anybody tell you differently," Jeff said.

"If I had any delusions about the danger, you took those away today."

"That couldn't be helped," Jeff said.

"It was unexpected."

"I guess Hong Le didn't expect it either," I said.

"Just be ready on Friday so we don't have any more surprises."

"I'd still feel better if we gave this to the boss."

"The boss won't get this until it's done."

"It might be too late by then."

"That's a chance we'll have to take."

"That's fine for you to say. It's not your ass on the line."

"And what a pretty ass it is," Jeff said.

The plan was to arrive at the meeting half an hour early, bust Roger, and then get out of there. If all went right, we'd be out of there, with Roger in cuffs, before the other girls arrived.

Friday morning rolled around quickly, and I got up an hour before my usual time to get ready.

I arrived at the meeting place forty minutes before the scheduled time and was ready for whatever happened. I was dressed like a slut, and knew it.

I walked into the room where Roger was.

"What are you doing here so early?" he asked.

I flashed more skin than I felt comfortable doing, and said, "Eager to get going. Actually, I'm kind of excited about it."

He leered at me. "Almost makes me want to be an inmate," he said, and I felt like he was only half kidding.

Ten minutes later, Jeff arrived, dressed much like he was the first time. He held a brick of heroin in his hand. "You got the money?" he asked Roger.

Roger nodded, and gestured toward a briefcase on his desk. "All there," he said. "Just like we agreed on."

"Good," Jeff said, then he pulled out his gun and shot Roger twice in the chest.

"What the fuck!" I said. "What did you shoot him for?"

"He saw me kill Hong Le," Jeff said. "Can't live with that."

"And where does that leave me?"

Jeff put his gun away, and said, "You're smarter than him. You won't talk."

I waited until he had finished holstering his weapon, then walked to the desk where Roger sat, slumped over. I picked up Roger's gun—from his desk drawer—and pumped two shots into Jeff's chest. He fell with an astonished look on his face.

"You're right," I said. "I won't say a word."

I cleaned the gun of prints, then tossed it on the floor. After making sure the area was clean, I ran to change clothes.

They'd get nothing off the gun. It was untraceable, and it had no prints on it—with the exception of Roger's, which I conveniently placed back on the grip.

I went into the back room and changed into the uniform I had packed. I felt sure the noise from the shooting made someone call the cops, and I wanted to be ready to greet them. After all, Marc Jefferson deserved my full attention, woman-beating scum that he was. I only hoped in that last second he realized who it was that was pumping bullets into his chest—and why.

I was always surprised he never recognized me anyway. I thought he did that one time, but I brushed it off as casual recognition from the academy, and he went for it.

CHAPTER 13
CLEANING UP THE MESS

As predicted, I heard the sirens for the radio cars within minutes. Fortunately, I had come prepared and was now fully dressed in my uniform. Before long, the first officers burst through the door, wielding guns.

I stood still, hands in the air, not wanting to risk any mistakes. I had called it in as an "officer down," so they came prepared for trouble.

"I'm on the job," I said, though they should have been able to tell that from the uniform.

The lieutenant arrived a few minutes later. He looked around the room, knelt to check on Jeff, then stared in my direction. "What happened here?"

I gulped. "Jeff picked me up, as usual, except it was in his car instead of the patrol car. I thought that was odd, and asked him about it, but he said he needed to drop off the car to get fixed.

Anyway, we were driving down Eddy and he spotted a group of gang bangers running into the building. He pulled to the curb, hollered, 'Stay in the car,' and took off after them.

"Maybe ten minutes elapsed before I heard gunshots. I got out of the vehicle, and ran toward the sound of the shots. By the time I got here, Jeff and the other guy were down. I saw what looked to be teenagers running out the back. I called this in, then gave pursuit, but they were gone."

"Do you know this man?" the lieutenant asked, pointing toward Roger.

"Never saw him," I said. "And since you'll probably ask—no, I don't know why Jeff wasn't in uniform. He was dressed that way when he picked me up."

"Did you get a good enough look to pick them out of a lineup?"

"No. I only saw them from the back, and that was from a distance. I could try though."

"Go back to the station. Write up what happened, and be prepared for a lot of questions. *A lot.*"

I stared at him. "Look, I was doing my job. I have no idea what the hell went on here, but looking at the scene, it was a lot more than a few gangbangers being chased."

"No doubt," he said. "Now, get going."

The lieutenant grabbed my arm before I left. "Why didn't you take the money?" He pointed to a duffel bag full of cash next to Roger.

"It wasn't mine," I said.

He smiled. "That will go a long way in showing you had no part in this."

I headed back to the station, but turned on Larkin. I saw Binh on the corner with a few of his boys. I pulled over and rolled the window down. "What's up, Skinny?"

"Better cut that shit out, or I'll start calling you Millie."

I laughed. "You get what you needed?" I asked.

He tapped the inside pocket on his leather coat. "Enough cash to keep me going for a long time," he said. "How about you?"

"Officer Marc Jefferson is dead," I said. "It's been a long time coming, but now my mom and sister can rest. And so can everybody else he came into contact with, including his wife and child."

"Did he hurt them?" Binh asked.

"Last time I saw her, she had a broken arm, and the kid had too many bruises for a five-year-old."

Binh shook his head. "Easy enough to kill a man, but to hit your own blood is nasty, especially your own kid."

He took a sip of coffee, and looked in my direction. "You've done good for yourself, kid. I never would have guessed it."

"Wouldn't have been possible without you," I said. "If you hadn't found Lisa Benz's body, I never would have gone to school, and I wouldn't have made the academy."

"Funny how things turn out," Binh said. "You, a cop. Who would have figured it?"

"I'm not staying a cop," I said. "I did what I wanted to do. Now, it's time to move on."

"Where are you going?" he asked.

"Don't know yet. Maybe Dallas. Maybe Houston. For some reason I feel drawn to Texas."

"I'll look in on your mom and sister," Binh said. "Drop a few flowers now and then."

A tear rolled down my cheek. "That would be great, Binh." I got out of the car and gave him a hug. "Nothing would make me happier."

It took a week to straighten out the mess with Jeff, but then I was free. Some people might have been bothered by what I did, but not me. I felt good. That son of a bitch had taken advantage of my mom and us for years. But no more. He wouldn't take advantage of anyone again.

One week later, I quit the force and started packing. I didn't have much to take besides clothes, but I did want the clothes.

Since I spoke to Binh last, I had settled on Houston, so I had a long way to go—five days of driving if I calculated right.

I just hoped the city lived up to my expectations.

OTHER BOOKS COMING SOON

Fiction

A Promise of Vengeance (Fantasy)
My first fantasy, and the first book in a four-book series—the Rules of Vengeance. (Three are already written and the fourth is being outlined.)

Murder Is Invisible ### (going through editing)
Frankie and Nicky are back.

Non-Fiction

- No Mistakes Grammar, Volume I, Misused Words. (being proofread)
- No Mistakes Grammar, Volume II, Misused Words for Business (being proofread)
- No Mistakes Grammar, Volume III, More Misused Words. (being proofread)
- No Mistakes Writing, Writing Shortcuts (being proofread)
- Uneducated—Thirty-Seven People Who Redefined the Definition of Education (being proofread)
- Whiskers and Bear—Volume I of the Life on the Farm Series (sent to editor)

Children's Books

- No Mistakes Grammar for Kids, Volume I—Much and Many (Sent to editor)
- No Mistakes Grammar for Kids, Volume II—Lie and Lay (Sent to editor)
- No Mistakes Grammar for Kids, Volume III—Then and Than (Sent to editor)
- Shinobi Goes to School—Life on the Farm for kids. (working on illustrations)

Get on the mailing list and you'll be sure to be notified of release dates and sales. Mailing list

ACKNOWLEDGMENTS

I wish to once again thank all of the phenomenal help I've received from Tirr and their magnificent team of therapists.

I especially want to thank Clayci for her undying support and enthusiasm. It has been a tremendous help.

As always, I give more thanks than I can muster to my loving wife, Mikki. You're the best. And you have been the best for forty-seven years.

ABOUT THE AUTHOR

 Giacomo (Jim) Giammatteo is a headhunter and has done retained searches in the medical device/ diagnostics & biotech/pharma industries for 30 years. He successfully completed more than 500 assignments, and he evaluated, edited, and wrote thousands of résumés. Giacomo has also interviewed and done reference checks on more than 1,000 candidates.

As if that wasn't enough to put him into a small room with padded walls, Giacomo is also a bestselling author of several mystery/suspense novels, including: Murder Takes Time, Murder Has Consequences, and Murder Takes Patience in the Friendship & Honor series; and A Bullet For Carlos, Finding Family, and A Bullet From Dominic in the Blood Flows South series. Other fiction includes Necessary Decisions, Old Wounds, and Promises Kept (coming soon), in the Redemption Series.

His non-fiction work includes No Mistakes Resumes, Book I of No Mistakes Careers, as well as book II—No Mistakes Interviews.

He has also written the No Mistakes Grammar Series, No Mistakes Writing, No Mistakes Publishing, No Mistakes Grammar for Kids, and How to Select a Self-publishing Service, Uneducated, and the Life on the Farm Series for both kids and adults. Giacomo's first fantasy series—the Rules of Vengeance—is coming soon.

In his spare time, Giacomo and his wife run an animal sanctuary with 45 loving "friends."

www.ingramcontent.com/pod-product-compliance
Lightning Source LLC
Chambersburg PA
CBHW071840190726
48292CB00005B/1844